Novels by Elizabeth Savage

Summer of Pride
But Not for Love
A Fall of Angels
Happy Ending
The Last Night at the Ritz
A Good Confession
The Girls from the Five Great Valleys
Willowwood

Willowwood

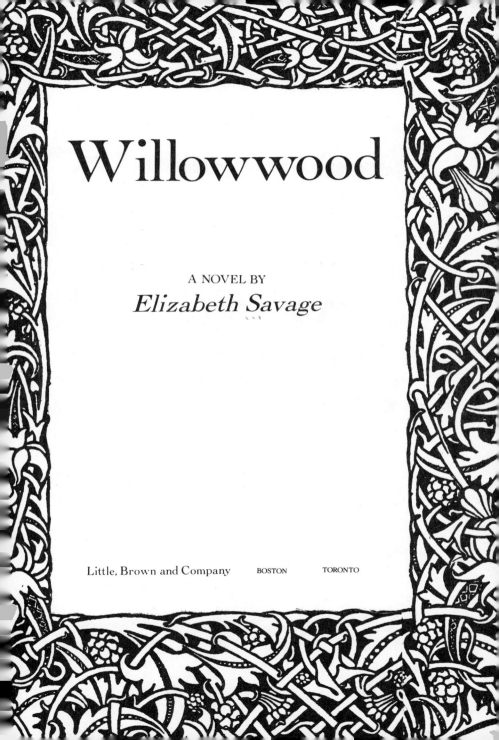

Willowwood

A NOVEL BY

Elizabeth Savage

Little, Brown and Company   BOSTON   TORONTO

Third Printing
T 08/78

Library of Congress Cataloging in Publication Data

Savage, Elizabeth.
  Willowwood.

    1. Rossetti, Dante Gabriel, 1828–1882, in fiction,
drama, poetry, etc. 2. Rossetti, Mrs. Elizabeth
Eleanor (Siddal), d. 1862—Fiction.   I.   Title.
PZ4.S263Wi   [PS3569.A823]   813'.5'4   78-7866
ISBN 0-316-77138-4

DESIGNED BY D. CHRISTINE BENDERS

*Published simultaneously in Canada
by Little, Brown & Company (Canada) Limited*

PRINTED IN THE UNITED STATES OF AMERICA

This one for Tom

"O ye, all ye that walk in Willowwood,
   That walk with hollow faces burning white;
What fathom-depth of soul-struck widowhood,
   What long, what longer hours, one lifelong night,
Ere ye again, who so in vain have wooed
   Your last hope lost, who so in vain invite
Your lips to that their unforgotten food,
   Ere ye, ere ye again shall see the light! . . ."

DANTE GABRIEL ROSSETTI

I

Lizzie

1

HER NAME WAS NOT really Fanny Cornforth.

Her name was really Sarah Cox, but since she had a habit of appropriating that which she preferred, she took the name — and had a right to it in a way, because Cornforth was the name of a great-aunt before her. This aunt had been an actress and although actresses are not highly regarded, Fanny had thought to be one because noblemen want to set you up in luxury. But that was when she was twelve. Now that she is sixteen she knows she is too lazy for it. For the stage, that is.

Behold her on this autumn afternoon: she stands under the arch at the doors of the Royal Academy schools, and she is watching the young men come and go. In particular, she looks for one. Her husband teases her but does not mind, because they are all artists over there and have no money. Mr. Hughes (such is her husband's name) is a porter by trade and runs errands for those who attend the schools. The painters are more forgetful than the sculptors (perhaps their materials are easier to forget) and are always sending out for paper and for art gum. Fanny sits for the Life class.

It was there that she met the precocious John Millais, who had been admitted to the august establishment when he was nine, and Holman Hunt of the great blond beard and the iron morality, and their friend Dante Gabriel Rossetti, who hangs about but no longer attends because he quit when they would not advance him from the Antique into the Life. He refers to the eminent founder as Sir Sloshua Reynolds. It is Dante Gabriel she is waiting for as she leans, cracking walnuts in her strong white teeth. Here he comes.

Arms akimbo now under the rough shawl that guards her plump shoulders from the prying autumn wind, she tosses the weight of her wheat-coloured hair.

"Hey!" Fanny calls.

He has dark curls and burning eyes and likes the ladies, but Fanny is not his type.

"Whyn'cha paint me?" she says. "I'll sit for free."

"You're not my type," he says.

Fanny's laugh wells from a soft, deep throat. She says, "Want to bet?"

It is this kind of flirting that distresses Holy Hunt and makes Ford Madox Brown fear that their young friend Gabriel is not serious. The fact of his Italian blood is to them no excuse: if anything, that should make him more careful of appearances. About Fanny Cornforth's unsuitability, however, Rossetti is quite serious; the women whom he paints are spirituelle; a breath would carry them away; they have no legs.

But he likes Fanny because she has no side and spills her friendliness as easily as Flora scatters flowers, and because she is a big, strong girl, bright-coloured and abundant, and because she amuses him.

"Next time I need a bacchante," he says, "I'll call on you."

"Do that," she says. "What's a bacchante?"

Her husband is old and Gabriel is young; his glance is hot and the black, bright eyes promise mischief. Like a child in a toy shop, she decides. *I want this one.* She laughs aloud and hurls at him a handful of walnut shells, and as he hurries off to Charlotte Street he does not know that one shell, like a tiny boat, rides on the dark waves of his hair.

Annus mirabilis! In 1850 great winds were rising that would sweep away the England that Gabriel Rossetti knew, but like many a man when the big winds rise, he saw only the loose leaves that blew about the streets. He had noted that plans were in progress for the Crystal Palace, although the Great Exhibit would not open for another four years. The sovereign — a happy woman, then — was safely delivered of Arthur William Patrick Albert, Duke of Connaught, and the gentry rejoiced while the poor cursed another expense upon the crown. *David Copperfield* concluded, and all England wept over the fading of the Child-Wife — except for Gabriel Rossetti and his friends. They were too elevated for Mr. Dickens and too dedicated and, in short, too grand.

But *In Memoriam* was different. Mr. Tennyson was made Laureate by his grateful Queen and over the Laureate's lament for Arthur Hallam, they shed private tears.

> My Arthur, whom I shall not see
> Till all my widow'd race be run;
> Dear as the mother to the son,
> More than my brothers are to me.

This they understood, for Gabriel and his friends loved one another.

That had been a fine year for the Pre-Raphaelite Brotherhood (for so, in jest, they called themselves); they had tweaked the lion's tail. Now this was the dearest wish of each of them: to mock the aesthetic taste of their elders and to replace the dark, loose oils of the Academicians with their own closely observed, bright, tender, tale-telling canvases.

And this was at a time when Friedrich Engels had brought forth his terrible indictment of an industrial society? Yes. They were generous young men, they were gifted young men, they were uninformed young men. Not one of them knew that in the sacred name of laissez-faire children were harnessed like animals in the mines and on their hands and knees dragged trucks through passages but eighteen inches high. With their own eyes they saw the muddy portraits — the noble, anthropomorphic stags and sentimental dogs; they did not see the children.

Oh, a fine year for the PRB! They had published a small magazine called *The Germ* in which they denounced tradition and for which they had been hysterically attacked by both *The Athenaeum* and *The Times* — no small feat for lads still in their twenties. Triumphantly, to show they held no traffic with commerce or with convention, they went beardless and wore their hair below their collars. It was a fashion more becoming to Gabriel than to the rest of them, whose fair English locks refused to tumble with Italianate profusion like his; neither did their eyes glow with that dark fire.

The household on Charlotte Street toward which Gabriel now hurried (Gabriel was always hurried) was an odd one; at least most people chose to find it so. The Rossettis were poor! Furthermore, they were of foreign and eccentric stock, and even the ladies of the family could read and write in Latin and made no effort to conceal it.

The father was a patriot and a scholar who had been exiled from Italy for championing the defeated, having stood for Napoleon when Napoleon fell and for the Carbonari when Ferdinand of Naples withdrew the frail new constitution and exiled everyone. Nevertheless, there was named for him in his birthplace the Piazza Gabriele Rossetti. He was a proud, though impoverished, man.

The mother was a Polidori; one of her brothers had challenged Shelley to a duel and had been personal physician to Lord Byron; when dismissed by that fickle genius he had withdrawn from the Continent to England, where he poisoned himself in a pique. The mother, perhaps in reaction to such impulsiveness and perhaps because she was half English, had cultivated a silent strength and had become the staff of the family. This was just as well, since her spouse, as professor of Italian at King's College, received a stipend of only ten pounds a year. When he was not teaching he spent his time proving, to his own satisfaction, that *The Divine Comedy* was Masonic propaganda which, while disguised for safety's sake, was directed toward the freedom of rational man and the destruction of the Church. Saint John, Saint Paul, John Bunyan, and John Milton he found to have been fellow conspirators; Victor Hugo, too.

Meantime the mother trudged from private Italian lesson to private Italian lesson as, after a brief bout as a governess, did the eldest child, Maria. The youngest, William Michael, went as a boy into the Excise Office. Christina was too unhappy and too delicate to do more than help around the house, and Dante Gabriel did little but show promise.

But such promise! Always his father's favourite, Gabriel was precocious and rebellious, refusing any useful activity save art and literature and any formal instruction in either of these. The old revolutionary admired his son's spirit and also his flashing eyes and floating hair. He often quoted to himself:

> For he on honey-dew hath fed,
> And drunk the milk of Paradise.

But then, he admired all his children. Maria was so reserved, Christina so intense, and both of them so pious! Though he himself fiercely rejected piety, he thought it pretty in a woman. And William Michael was dependable. But the father did have to admit that when they were all at home together, they crammed the small sitting room where the whole family lived and worked and ate. And then, every night there were visitors — many of them distinguished, a few famous and a few mad, and most of them in real need of the bread and coffee that was all the household could proffer.

When Gabriel ran lightly up the steps at Charlotte Street, chafing his hands because the evening had turned cold, he found Maria in the hall. She greeted her brother with a distant kindliness that recognized him as a child of God. Before she glided to her garret and presumably to her devotions, she murmured to him, "It's the thirteenth."

Gabriel slapped his brow. "Of course," he said. "I had forgotten."

More quietly than was his wont, he entered the sitting room, where a small fire glowed bravely in the grate. The room was pleasant enough, but whether it were well kept or ill, who could tell? There was too much in it. Most of this, in one shape or another, consisted of paper, so much of which abounded that one could only hazard a guess at what lay underneath. Like any serious man of letters the old gentleman would not permit his table to be touched — except at teatime, when he was resigned to yield one small corner. The overflow was piled in loose and leaning towers, and over all and in between there was scattered a confetti of ink spots where the great man had dipped and shaken his pen in the frenzies of his composition. And then there were the books. Unfortunately for the sake of order, in that house everybody read.

Frances Mary Lavinia Polidori Rossetti sat beside the fire to guard it from the excesses of her impractical mate. She lifted her hooded eyes, smiled sternly at her son, and pointed to the chair beside her.

She raised her finger to her lips. "It's the thirteenth," she said.

And of October, which explained the gloom of the master and his guests. One was a costermonger with a proud and noble name. One claimed to be a ruminant because he believed himself to have two stomachs; he was an expert on quattrocento brocades. One was John Hookham Frere.

Frere was a man of wealth who had for years encouraged the Poet of the Revolution with cold cash. More important to the Poet was Frere's staunch belief in the Conspiracy, to the roster of which he had added Petrarch and Pico della Mirandola. Having at first taken fire, Frere had recently lost heart and was now paying Gabriele not to publish, lest religion totter and timid mothers cancel the Italian lessons that he gave their young.

Gabriele Rossetti was a beautiful old man, much older than his wife, with fine eyes that were fading (he was almost blind). The bony structure behind the explosive brows was plainly marked — the Bar of Michelangelo, the world calls that, and knows it for the brand of genius. Dante Gabriel had it, too.

Tonight, while the old man and his visitors sat in attitudes of dejection, Christina stood bowed over her work at her tall, narrow writing desk. She had looked up briefly when her brother entered, but though she had frowned it was not at all sure that she had seen him. The brothers and sisters had developed amazing powers of concentration. They had had to.

If she had indeed frowned because she saw Gabriel, it might have been that she was still troubled by *The Germ*. Christina had opposed it at the start, alarmed that the little journal might encourage revolutionary politics and irreverence, although she had herself contributed to its pages four poems which some might think unwholesome, dwelling as they did upon sunless rivers and moribund maidens. Or might it have been that she feared her brother's influence upon Mr. Collinson?

James Collinson had been received into the PRB because of Gabriel's enthusiasm for *The Charity Boy's Debut*, in which a ragged boy is shown absorbed into the workhouse. Gabriel, when he had painted the Virgin cowering on her bed before an implacable angel, had covered her feet, but that was not because he was not interested in her toes — only that he could not paint them. Now Collinson had rendered every pore in the brutal faces of the attendants, every crack in the broken shoes that the boy wore, and every splinter in the dirty floor. Since then, Collinson had done nothing much except to court Christina.

Because of a natural lethargy which, to be frank, resembled that of the Fat Boy, one might not have thought that Collinson would appeal to Christina Rossetti, but apparently even superior young women would prefer to be courted than not. And then too, it was rumoured that Christina was about to win a great moral victory because James Collinson, a devout Roman Catholic, was considering the Church of England: to reverse a pious man is an achievement, and Christina may have feared the influence of her irreverent brother upon her apostate. She raised her head,

with its smooth bands of hair, and from the hooded eyes
so like her mother's shot Gabriel a baleful look.

Then Gabriele Rossetti elevated his steel spectacles and
his noble head in its black skullcap and announced, "It was
the act of a man of honour."

For it was the anniversary of the very day upon which
an old friend — overcome by personal humiliation and to
protest the execution of Joachim Murat, the "Dandy King"
of Naples — had slit his throat. He who thought the gesture excessive did not possess the Italian fire.

"I should have been proud to follow his example," said
the father, "were it not for the responsibility of my beloved family."

Since the interesting event had taken place in 1815,
before the beloved family had been contemplated, this was
a singular instance of the Poet's Vision; but the annual
tribute having now been accomplished, the old friends
about the table cheered and the whole room warmed and
brightened.

And then William Michael, kindly and urbane though
but a boy in years, came home from the Excise Office and
Maria, a distant Hebe, produced the steaming brew.

And Dante Gabriel, rising so quickly that his dark locks
flew about his shoulders, cried, "Where is Will Little?
Demme, I told him to meet me here. Where's Will?"

OBSERVE THIS little person.

Dapper and neat as he can be, he buttons his waistcoat, fastens his little yellow gloves. He is twenty-two and lives in lodgings by himself rather than with his lady mother, who does not mind, knowing him to be of tidy manners and more ordered habits than some of those among his circle. By this she means Dante Gabriel Rossetti, whose habits are not orderly. That does not mean she would not like to know the Rossettis. Just to hear about them is as good as a book.

"Do you think they would like to come to tea?" she had once asked.

"No," her son had said.

Beneath the high points of his collar his cravat is quiet-coloured, his pumps gleam, a short cloak hangs over his jacket from his well-brushed shoulders; he is disciplined. And yet — he snaps shut the chased cover of his handsome watch — he may be late. If he is late, Gabriel will not like it.

His name is William Little. Little Will, Gabriel calls
him, and he does not mind, though he would not countenance the soubriquet from any other soul. Nor need he.
Glance about these rooms, in which all has been glossed,
rubbed, shaken and aired. He does not, of course, do this
himself, nor does his mother feel required to supervise.
For all his diminutive size, his landlady knows him for a
martinet. Yet his will trembles before that of his friend.

A manly love ennobles: Will Little loves his friend.
Mr. Wilde not having yet ripped the mask of reticence
from the grimace of an antique vice, he is not afraid that
such love be misinterpreted. Oh, late! Down the stairs he
trots into a blustery London night.

Fearful as he may be of being late, he is more fearful
that in spite of his imperious summons, Gabriel may not
be there at all. Since Gabriel left the Academy he has also
for the most part left home to work around in the studios
of those among his friends who can afford him. These arrangements never last long because his friends tire of his
charm and of his raids upon their supplies. They also tire
of his disdain and of the way in which, baffled by his own
inadequacies, he throws himself upon the floor and sulks.
Gabriel is not known for his patience.

Yes, late! Perhaps more than most, Will is moved by
the Laureate's threnody:

> He past; a soul of nobler tone:
>> My spirit loved and loves him yet,
>> Like some poor girl whose heart is set
> On one whose rank exceeds her own.

Of course Alfred, Lord Tennyson, did have the comfort
that his friend had indeed passed. Will Little's friend must
still be placated. But as he scurries down the street Will's
heart is high, because he hopes to bear a gift fit to placate
a hero. He does not know his gift will prove as dire as

that poisoned shirt which Deianira gave her husband, Hercules.

There he goes, leaning into the wind that nips at the corners of his cloak and turns them back so that a passerby may see — and find both pleasant and edifying — the nice silk of its lining. But there are not many passersby tonight, either in his own neighborhood or here where the streets are dark and wet, for those who make their livings on these streets — the cheap-jacks, running patterers, the flower girls, the crossing sweepers, the ring sellers and fortune-tellers — have all withdrawn to the flatty kens where they will crowd together for the night: men, women, and children mingled with few beds and fewer covers. Now and again some lady of the night may hurry by, seeking the lights of Seven Dials and the prospect of her trade.

It is these doxies Will is seeking.

Not for himself! Certainly not! He seeks them for his friend and, if Gabriel should care to share, for the friends of his friend. For they all have trouble finding models. They are too poor to afford fees and have used up their mothers and their sisters; other nice women will not sit for them, since everyone knows how artists are. But the young women of easy virtue find the task amusing; they are not afraid to be in studios and they like the young men. They will allow any number to draw from them, in any role, and will take their pay in beer and laughter.

So whenever Will walks abroad he looks for models, and it is never easy — so many of the girls are coarse, slack-postured, and foulmouthed. It is because of this that tonight he wishes to observe a certain bonnet shop where (he has been told) there are pretty working girls. Not that he confuses working girls with drabs, but it is sensible to feel that working girls would not be working, were they gently bred; therefore he may find someone suitable. He likes to do these little things for Gabriel, who may be grateful, and he is aware that to maintain his place in Gabriel's group he must earn his way, since he himself is not an artist, although he is an appreciator and fancies himself a critic. Then too, he is never quite sure of Gabriel's affection for him — or for anybody else.

Except for his parents. And Will too, who reveres that strange and passionate household, is always pleased to please the old Rossettis, who tensely appreciate any appreciation of their gifted son.

No, he thinks, peering through the shadows (the gaslights bob). Is this the street? This is the street. No, the members of the PRB are not dissolute. In fact, they are rather stern young men. And yet Will knows uneasily that many people might — and, in fact, do — consider Gabriel's interest in these unfortunate girls unwholesome. His curiosity about their deplorable days goes beyond his interest in the play of light and shadow upon their poor worn bodies. Will had himself been present on the evening when Gabriel read to his assembled family from a new poem, *Jenny*. (Gabriel has never known whether he is a poet or a painter: this will make for trouble.)

> Lazy laughing languid Jenny,
> Fond of a kiss and fond of a guinea . . .

It was not a poem anyone would easily forget, but Will especially remembered it because of Christina. Much of the circumlocution was pretty and without offense.

> Like a rose shut in a book
> In which pure women may not look . . .

But Gabriel, who lacked his sister's fierce religiosity, liked to tease. He should not have continued with those verses in that company but he did, nor did he hesitate when he reached the distressing lines:

> Have seen your lifted silken skirt
> Advertise dainties through the dirt . . .

His mother, a true Roman matron, did not so much as raise her eyes from the embroidery upon her lap. But Christina Rossetti arose.

"Fie!" she said. And then she drew her skirts about her and left the room.

Will Little does not see how she could have done otherwise.

He is not fond of Christina, who has a very caustic way of speaking. There are many who think her beautiful and he supposes that she is, in a gaunt, burning sort of way. But anyone who thinks the shy white moth of a girl who receives in fear the Annunciation in Gabriel's *Ecce Ancilla Domini* resembles Christina Rossetti is mistaken.

She does not like him, either.

But although Will is a little afraid of Christina, he is more afraid not to please his friend. Therefore he tolerates now the wind that whips his trouser legs around his ankles and the rain that insinuates itself under his collar and even the company of two other young men — bloods, dandies — who lie in wait for the young women and who may, humiliating thought, consider Will there for no more elevating reason than their own. And the girls are pretty, as Will can see through the brightly lighted window, though given to giggles and to a tendency to glance outside and then to poke one another. Well, the streets are dark and muddy and even dangerous, and a girl has little fun and may be excused if she accepts the escort of a young gentleman and perhaps a plate of oysters and a glass of something along the way. Now one by one they slip out of the door with bonnets over their curls and pattens on their little feet.

Will does not glance at them. He is looking at the last

girl left inside the shop. She is reaching up to put a bonnet box upon a shelf and the line of her slender body is exquisite. She turns and for a moment looks blindly out into the night. Surely she cannot see him, but he will never forget this first moment in which he sees her.

She has wise, grey, thoughtful eyes in a face of great delicacy. This is no pretty poppet but a beautiful young woman, grave and gracious — and her head is covered with folds of heavy, shining, rose-gold hair.

His heart beats fast inside his little coat.

That it should be he to bring this treasure to Gabriel! Youth to youth, beauty to beauty, magic to genius — she is the first female he has seen worthy of his friend. It is not for this one to pose as a country maiden cozened and betrayed and to be paid with a shilling and a dram. She and Gabriel will meet solemnly. She will become his Guinevere, his Iseult, his Beatrice. And all because of him!

Observe this little person closely: he is dangerous.

Ah, Will, Will, cannot you see the angel of destruction hovering over the dark head, over the golden one?

3

ELIZABETH ELEANOR SIDDAL was no drab or doxie, but a young woman of great powers and with the instincts of a gentlewoman, to which she had some claim.

True, that her father was a cutler, his father an optician, and *his* father a scissors-grinder — ah, but he of the generation before that, by embroiling himself in litigations had tumbled the family fortunes. To that day, proof positive of blue blood lay in the registers of the town of Hope, wherein it was written that a Jacobus Sudel, of Norman stock, had wed an Anna Grant de Hope, and that of their issue one had married into the even older family of Greaves. There was a Greaves, a knight of Beeley, as late as the time of Henry III, and it was from the Greaves that the gold and acres (later lost) had come.

No wonder Lizzie Siddal held her head so high.

Upon a table in her humble home on the Kent Road there lay a red morocco volume that bore the family coat of arms: three birds and the word *Honour*. And the Siddals had the right to quarter that of Greaves: *Per Bend et Gules*, and with an eagle displayed.

Her mother, who had been a mere Miss Evans out of Wales, brooded more about these past glories than did her ineffectual father, who fiddled of evenings and played the organ in the chapel on the Euston Road. All of the women in her mother's family had those strange eyes and the hair like spoiled gold. What had it done for them? Precious little.

Lizzie's oldest sister had married a baker. She had two other sisters, one of whom was flighty, and three brothers, one of whom was simple. She herself would not settle for a baker, nor could she much longer live at home with all of them except the baker's wife. At fourteen, she had been apprenticed to the bonnet maker. How could her mother have done that to a poet?

Easily. The household needed her wages and Mrs. Tozer was a personal friend and had vowed that Lizzie should not be harassed or seduced.

But she need not have vowed. Elizabeth Siddal was courteous to the coarse girls with whom she worked, her cold and pretty manners pleased the clientele, and her twenty-four pounds a year earned her at home the right to the garret, which was in turn too hot and too cold for anyone else. And there she wrote the little verses about damsels and knights that had run through her shining head ever since; bringing butter home from market, she had read a poem of Tennyson's on the oily paper that had been used to wrap it:

> With blackest moss the flower-plots
> Were thickly crusted, one and all:
> The rusted nails fell from the knots
> That held the pear to the gable-wall.

Meantime she grew thinner and began to take drops for a little cough. Her mother's neighbor wished to know had there not been consumption in the family? Her mother denied. But after that she refused Lizzie a fire, in order to discourage her from spending all that time up there alone.

Though really, there was not all that much time. Lizzie rose early; that was not the worst time of the day. The mist rose from the river and when the sun struck pure above the bloated dogs and flotsam, if you kept up your head you only saw the sun. Except in the Season, she went home at dusk. During the Season the great ladies had to tend their heads and the angle of a feather or the fall of a ribbon could keep Lizzie up until dawn. But dawn was safe. No one was up and about except the blear-eyed men who had to work but were not rested, and none of them were looking for a slap and tickle. Those who sought that were long since slapped and tickled.

Nobody wanted to tickle Lizzie anyhow. She was too aloof and too superior and she didn't look much like good sport. They preferred the reddened cheeks of the other girls to the rose that flamed, hectic, in Lizzie's white face. She often wondered if her mother knew that Mrs. Tozer pandered to the bloods. The girls couldn't live on what she paid them, so she supplied a showcase in which they could display the tawdry charms that would win them a carefree year or two and a bottle of the bubbly.

But Elizabeth had to marry, because she was not fitted to be a whore. Meantime she became seventeen.

Lizzie had never had any money, in spite of her father's papers that proved she should have had; she was not interested in money. If she had dreams (she did have dreams) they were of a young man, well bred and distinguished and pure and of fine family and exquisite manners, who would be strong of heart to find and then to claim his lady.

Meantime the endless days crept by. Those who had married bakers were in childbed, but Lizzie would have no baker and no butcher's boy and no hostler. But the troubled and troubling words of Mariana lapped at her mind, insistent as the river:

> . . . but most she loathed the hour
> When the thick-moted sunbeam lay
> Athwart the chambers, and the day
> Was sloping toward his western bower.

And sometimes in her garret, pushing the paper petulantly from her, she would lift the bright burden of her hair with her white fingers.

> "He cometh not," she said;
> She said, "I am aweary, aweary,
> I would that I were dead!"

That morning began badly.

As Lizzie descended in the dark the narrow staircase with the worn, slanting steps, she heard her mother's voice raised in hysteria.

"Death in the house! Charles, get the broom!"

Lizzie froze with her long, white fingers at the throat of her grey gown. Her mother was superstitious; so was Lizzie. She heard her father's laboured breathing and the slap of the broom against the low walls. Her haughty mother claimed from the heritage of her Welsh blood her sensitivity to signs and omens, but one need not be Welsh to know that a bird in the house denotes the passing of a soul. Tomfoolishness, her father said — but then, he was not Welsh.

There is indeed something horrid about a bird trapped where it is not natural for it to be. This one beat frantically against wall and lintel, wings whirring, breast pulsating, tiny eyes fixed in fright, claws rigid. Her mother screamed and cowered. Her father thumped.

It was not the right time of year for birds nor the right time of day; the windows were tight and closed against the black fog, the door still barred, so her brothers and sisters still slept as if felled and had not slipped away upon mischief. The bird whirled near and Lizzie clutched her hair; it swooped away and her father with the flat of the broom beat it into the fireplace. Her mother darted forward and lit the fire.

Then taking a deep, shuddering breath, she looked at her daughter and said, "Your ear is showing."

Because Louis Napoleon thought that ears were ugly, the modish were not showing ears, but wore their hair in sleek bandeaux that curtained their cheeks and was done low in back in buns upon which their little bonnets rode.

"There," her mother said. "That is better."

Between the girl and her mother there was an uneasy truce. The mother was demanding, often harsh, always defensive of her dignity and the respect due her. She was a good housekeeper who kept polished to a silken glow the few good pieces left them, and in that tiny house although the cups were cracked, the tea was poured from silver. She was also vain and often let down her own extraordinary hair to prove it longer than her daughter's (and indeed though it was silver as the teapot, it reached her knees).

"Tomfoolishness," Charles Siddal said again, crossly.

No it wasn't. If a bird meant death to plain folk, how much more to Siddals! And Mrs. Siddal placed her hand upon the book that bore the family crest. Three birds!

When Lizzie was distressed the demon within pinched and clawed her stomach until she could have cried aloud. At such times she could not eat and if she had, could not have kept it down; this morning she turned her head from her mother's porridge. Mrs. Tozer would give her a cup of tea.

Wrapped in her long, grey mantle, Lizzie slipped into the early shadows. Those fortunates who lived across the river considered this a dubious side, inhabited by the slack, poor, and possibly dangerous, who crowded together in ramshackle dwellings without earth closets, and where families and transients slept together in questionable intimacy from which they tumbled into the street to drink and brawl. But this far out from the city, the Kent Road was not unpleasant. Here the road wandered and became half rural, the little buildings stood alone; some had a bit of grass and behind them hop fields stretched. Number 8, the Siddals, stood just across from the Asylum for Blind and Deaf Children, and next door to the Murderer.

The Murderer! When Lizzie escaped the Kent Road, she would not leave behind the memory of the Murderer. Mr. Greenacre had kept a candy shop and cut the throat of a laundress for her savings. Lizzie, whose mind was tenacious of the bizarre, shuddered to think of him not only because he had dismembered his victim and distributed her among the weirs and locks, but because with the very hand so horribly bloodied he had often taken her own small hand and led the little Siddal girl safely across the road. Long after he was executed (they said the hangman had to jump upon his shoulders) the child woke shrieking.

Nobody thought it morbid of her; it was not a family that looked on things as morbid. One of her brothers bought the dismembering knife and invited his sister to inspect it; the eight-year-old fainted. Gradually the shock wore off, or seemed to. But Lizzie to the end of her life often woke shrieking.

Oh, but this long day dragged. As the slow, pallid hours of morning crept by, Lizzie bent silently over her sewing; at noon when the others gobbled their thick bread and cheese, she took a cup of tea. During the endless after-

noon, Mrs. Tozer called her from the workroom to cope
with the ladies who came for fittings or the footmen who
came to collect and might well carry home the word that
the establishment was genteel. And she liked Lizzie to
try on the bonnets for the undecided; her figure, slim as a
stem and graceful as grass, and the glorious hair upon
which the bonnets sat lightly as butterflies, misled many
a matron. Once she swayed, and Mrs. Tozer looked sharply
at her waist and then smiled at her own concern. Not
Lizzie.

But Mrs. Tozer ran her thumb along her whiskery upper lip. She didn't like Lizzie's color — the flush that leaped
into that white, white skin. If the girl had consumption,
she would get rid of her. Everyone feared consumption,
and the coughs and fevers that decimated the lower
classes did not always decently stop there. Too many families counted among their early dead a son sent abroad
for the climate or a daughter pining and fading in an upper chamber. And nothing to be done for it but bleeding.
No, if Lizzie was ill her mother must take her back before the customers hesitated to touch the silks and velvets
that her long, slim fingers touched.

While it was true that the gilt and rose colouring was
lovely (and the strange almond, agate eyes) and that the
tall girl was courteous and gentle, the Lord helps only
those who help themselves. Mrs. Tozer had come up the
hard way.

All day, while the shadows danced their slow dance
until the weak lights of the lamps bleached the workroom,
Lizzie felt lonely and deprived. No one was to leave until
eight, but after seven, when Mrs. Tozer retired to the
small apartment that looked into the alley where she hung
her wash, the girls began to slip away. If no toff waited,
they would join their chaps, whose big red knuckles and
brutish jokes offended Lizzie. But what was there for her?

Nothing. Only the bare, cold garret and the scraps of paper on which she dreamed of him who should come and did not.

And then that very night, there he was.

She had wearily clasped her mantle high about her long, white neck, bent to lock the door, turned, and saw there underneath the gaslight two young men waiting for her. One was a neat little person and the other, a dark young god. His face was beardless, the ringlets of his dark hair brushed the shoulders of his cape, his eyes, which looked as if someone had smudged them with an inky thumb, were fiercely demanding and examined her as if she were a possession. He took her hand in his and drew her into the circle of the streetlight.

Elizabeth Eleanor Siddal was afraid of death and of the harbingers of death. She was afraid of no man.

He took the bonnet from her head and the big pins from the heavy knot and the massy red-gold of her hair spilled over her shoulders and almost to her hips. The young man slipped his warm, strong fingers beneath her hair and up to her cold neck and moved her head to left and right.

"Never bind your hair again," he said.

His voice was deep and musical and rich as velvet. For a long moment the dark Italian eyes and the cold English ones looked at each other calculatingly.

"I am a painter," he said. "You must sit for me."

No decent girl would sit for a painter and no timid one for a stranger.

"Well," he demanded impatiently, "will you come?"

Lizzie Siddal was only afraid of not living her life.

"Yes," she said.

4

LITTLE WILL LITTLE runs briskly up the three flights of stairs that lead to Number 14, Chatham Place, where Gabriel and William Michael have in common the leasehold of what Gabriel (but not in his brother's hearing) calls his crib. No longer does he drift from friend to friend distributing confusion but lives alone and revels in it, as do his friends. They are of an age at which they wish to escape their parents' roofs and the attention which accompanies those structures, and although they like to prowl the streets like a pride of lions they also need a place where they can smoke and mix their toddies when the weather worsens and where anyone momentarily overcome by spirits may, without comment, find temporary rest.

The building is old and hangs above the river, where the Fleet Street Ditch has just been filled, in an attempt to rid the neighborhood of the effluvium of discharged filth. However, the river still sends up a dank miasma that offends the casual visitor, but to which Gabriel and his friends have become accustomed. And the great stone edifice, rather resembling a fort, has compensations; not only do bow windows rise one above another to form towers, but Gabriel's rooms also boast a kind of terrace upon which, occasionally, Christina has had tea. She is too much the lady to remark on the stench that rises to her carved nostrils, or on the rags and drowned rats that swirl and bump below; and where else, pray, in this beehive of London, may one look across flowing water?

Gabriel has sold a painting to the Marchioness of Bath, who employs his aunt Charlotte Polidori and, like all artists, he assumes that from now on he will sell everything. If an ignorant public should not buy everything, his brother makes a steady income at the Excise Office, though the income is small and many calls are made on it. William Michael does not choose to live at Chatham Place but remains home with his parents and sisters, where in truth his company as well as his contribution is welcome.

William Michael does not care for Chatham Place. He does not like the smell nor the way Gabriel has somewhat furnished it with dusty hangings, broken furniture, and one fairly secure sofa upon which Gabriel himself habitually reclines, since when he is not actually brush in hand he reclines — he sees no sense in any posture between up and down. And William Michael does not like the other tenants. The lower floors of the building have no charm, but are labyrinthine, damp, and inconvenient, and by day are shared by old individuals who copy documents or of the goodness of their hearts loan money to the temporarily distressed. He only cares for it at night, when the PRB gathers to exchange the hot opinions which he, as secretary, records for posterity.

Gabriel likes it all, and being generous of temperament and averse to solitude, keeps open house for his friends; indeed, upon the rare occasions when he ventures forth during the good painting light, he leaves the key outside beneath the mat; his friends are to use the key and wait for him, so that he will not lose their company. So Will knocks smartly and then, as is the custom, tries the door.

The door is locked.

Disappointed, but far from crushed, he draws from his hand an immaculate glove, bends, taking great care not to disturb his trousers, and gingerly slides his hand under the dusty mat. There is no key there. Yet as he stands there confused and even a little hurt, he hears the soft, clandestine whisper of a skirt across the floor.

Rage fills his little bosom and turns his face white as his stock. That woman is in there. What kind of woman, pray, would visit a gentleman's rooms alone? With the door closed and locked? And for what purpose? And with what result? His friend, who has always made him welcome, welcomes him no more. How could he have been so mistaken about this bonnet maker? She is a witch, and with her carroty hair, heavy eyes, her little phthisic cough, and her proud and haughty airs (how could he ever have thought her beautiful?) she has bewitched his friend.

Even as he stands now, uncertain, he hears from within the low sound of muffled merriment, as if two clamp their hands across their mouths, with their eyes dancing into one another's.

And then impatiently his friend calls from within, "Go away! There's a good fellow!"

To Will Little, unappreciated and rejected, it is suddenly of the highest importance that Gabriel should not know which good fellow he has turned away and so, as filled with panic as if he were the guilty party, he scampers back down the stairs, and as his little boots patter softly, a high, bright peal of female laughter follows him.

Elizabeth Siddal has made an enemy.

Like many another, Will was dangerous because he thought that he knew best; unlike many another he had no pursuits to distract him from the implementation of what he thought was best. Also, he was dishonest, though he would have been shocked to be called so, and easily confused what he thought best for others with what he felt best for Will Little. Such people often set in motion currents which they cannot control and upon which small barks sail off into uncharted waters.

He had intended to supply Gabriel, and Gabriel alone, with a model — and with a model alone. Instead the woman was called The Sid, was acclaimed by all and sat for everyone, with Gabriel's tolerant consent, if at the time he did not require her services. It was the woman, not the model, he claimed for himself alone; how much he claimed, nobody cared to ask.

Furthermore, she was making money, more money than she had ever earned among her ribbons and laces. As a model the girl was patient and imaginative — she understood what each wanted and was willing to droop to such postures as they wished and to hold them, too; so patient was she that one might think she slept while posing were it not for the sudden slide of her green-ambery eyes under the rounded white lids. Nor did she question their demands, although their flights of fancy often wafted far. Young John Millais, with his mother's help, posed her in a bathtub as the drowning Ophelia, the better to observe the spiraling of her water-borne skirts and the copper tongues of her floating hair. It took hours and hours; the ingenious arrangement of lamps with which his mother had proposed to keep the water warm had not worked out, and Lizzie caught cold. What did that matter? One gets over colds.

She sat for Walter Deverell, the beautiful young man who in his strength and beauty was to die so soon — and for The Sid so conveniently, since his passion for her never could be questioned. She sat for grumbling Old Brown and in boy's clothes for the chaste Holman Hunt — and a creditable slim young man she made, if with more gentle grace than you are like to find in your hobbledehoy. For Gabriel, who had for the moment put aside the oils he had not learned to master, she sat for water-colours, and in these her long throat, queenly head, and look of cool disdain appear: *Rosso Vestita; Beatrice at a Marriage Feast Denying Dante Her Salutation; Guardami ben, ben son, ben son Beatrice.*

But the whole thing was getting out of hand. What Will had had in mind was that this girl could pose for Gabriel of a Sunday, glad to pick up two shillings and able to get herself home at night.

Instead, she had left home.

Since no woman leaves home unless she is debased, Will trembled for the morals of his friend, and his eyes dropped uneasily before the clear, accusing gaze of Christina. But they were wrong; Lizzie was far from debased. One toss of that regal head would stop the most innocent conversation; she strode Bohemia with the inviolate dignity of a queen. Perhaps in her unworldliness she simply did not see how equivocal her position became when she allowed Gabriel to find her rooms in Weymouth Street above a chemist's shop. True, both the landlord and his wife were of a granite respectability; true, that to these rooms she regularly repaired at night alone and proud in her independence.

And indeed she was so much in demand that Gabriel himself designed and had printed for her a professional card upon which, to commemorate that doughty Jacobus who had so triumphantly invaded the highborn Greaves, he had spelled her name newly, as *Sidal.*

"You must spell the name with only one *l* and one *d*," Gabriel told everyone, characteristically mistaken, "for she is a Sidal of Hope."

Nevertheless, the ladies would not meet her.

The doting mother of John Everett Millais permitted him to put her in the tub but when she emerged she was not asked to sup. And despite Walter Deverell's hot defense of Lizzie's superior mind and gifts, Mrs. Deverell had only asked if he perhaps might pose her in the garden. Because Mr. Deverell seldom entered the garden? His younger sisters had hidden behind bushes to giggle and peer.

Christina Rossetti no longer came for tea.

Nor, in spite of the weeping and warnings with which her mother had parted from her, did she at first even notice that she was not universally admired, so wonderful and adventurous did her new life seem. That she, whose days had been so leadenly routine — who seldom saw the brief suns of winter so red and small against a pewter sky, nor the full flare of a summer day scattered with green and peppered with hot light — should walk abroad at will and mingle with the people! Not in their sullen Sunday silences but eating, brawling, working; children at play in the gutters, girls proud in their ribbons, toffs in the park, and through it all the clop of horses' hooves, the cry of a vendor, the harsh, sweet strains of street organs, the rattle of life.

And gone was the garret where she had hidden, the weak circle of a bad lamp and the dry silence scratched only by a mouse in the wainscot. The little sitting room in Weymouth Street was bare, her basin chipped, the towels thin as gauze, but it was all her own and when Gabriel left her at the door, no one could enter with yawns and with complaints and with the order that she move over. For the first time in her life she slept alone. For the first time, unhindered, she stirred a bustling little fire and sat above it, stretching her long, thin fingers to the warmth till the blue veins showed through and then scribbling about betrayed maidens and repentant lovers or dreaming of the gaiety of the hours behind and that of those ahead.

Because when Gabriel dropped his brushes, threw the paint rags into the corner, and put on his worn velvet coat, they came — the knights of the Round Table. And she, their Guinevere, would sit untouched and cherished, smiling her small smile upon their pranks, their quips, their hot youth; and later from below her low lids she watched Gabriel make his magic on them as the firelight danced red on his dark curls and in that low, mellifluous voice he read of his own poems.

> The blessed damozel leaned out
> From the gold bar of Heaven;
> Her eyes were deeper than the depth
> Of waters stilled at even;
> She had three lilies in her hand,
> And the stars in her hair were seven.

Then he would raise his lustrous eyes to look upon her, and with a slight turn of her head she would shake the gilt glory of her hair about her shoulders. She was his Blessed Damozel. And she knew it.

So frail, so sweet to him that he would not permit the rough wind of heaven to visit her, but gathered her mantle tenderly about her throat and, when the gutters were aswirl, swung her across the gutters. To be sure, when he was painting he forgot her, allowed her to hold a pose until her shoulders ached and every muscle burned, and he forgot that she ate, as if she were so fey that she could live on dew and sunbeams. Both dew and sunbeams being hard to come by, she went without, and when he took her out to dine he did not notice her push aside the greasy fish on which he thrived.

None of that mattered, because he honoured her; never had he done more than touch her hand, though his look scorched her like a fire and kindled the flame in her bright cheeks. Soon he would speak, soon he would claim her, soon he would offer his hand in marriage and she would accept, and then his family would welcome her, as the new daughter in their house.

Meantime she rested secure in her pride and thought only with pleasure of the day when she would name as her true sister Christina, the poetess, to whose melodic, melancholy lines her heart responded.

> O EARTH, lie heavily upon her eyes;
>   Seal her sweet eyes weary of watching, Earth;
>   Lie close around her; leave no room for mirth
> With its harsh laughter, nor for sound of sighs.
> She hath no questions, she hath no replies . . .

For Collinson had got away.

And already, Elizabeth Siddal was as much in love with death as she was with love.

5

BUT GABRIEL WAS NOT matrimonially inclined.

How could he be? He had no income of his own and his name was still better known to his creditors than to the public. Aunt Charlotte bought a few pictures for herself, but it was not often that she could prevail upon her employer to do the same. He was still dependent upon the pocketbooks of his friends (and they on his, for Gabriel gave freely of what was given him) and upon his family, or rather, upon his younger brother, who dutifully recognized that genius must be served. Now he was not at all sure that William Michael, who so gladly contributed to the family, would be quite happy to assume the same role for a new family. He would hardly wish to continue paying rent on quarters which he did not inhabit even theoretically. No, that would probably be too much to ask.

And marriage, inevitably, meant a family; perhaps a large one. Nappies steaming by the fireplace, wailing scions, toddlers in the paint: whooping cough, measles, colic, and the nymph in a damp apron boiling onions. So perhaps it was domesticity to which Gabriel was not inclined, or would not have been had he seriously considered it at all, which he had not.

Nor did he accord a tittle's worth of thought to Mrs. Grundy. He was an artist; artists are not required to behave like other people. Furthermore, he had done nothing wrong. He had not so much as breathed upon her purity, and nothing had occurred which should make it impossible for his mother to receive Lizzie as his wife. But later, later! Meantime, like two innocent and lovely children, they gamboled in a meadow where only flowers and sweet airs abounded.

Besides, it had somehow come about that Fanny Cornforth, that big, cheery girl who posed for him when a Martha rather than a Mary was needed, had also begun to share with him her favours and his pleasures. About Fanny, the question of marriage could not arise.

Then a small feather of a cloud rose fluttering on the blue horizon of that joyous meadow; so small and so ephemeral that Gabriel promptly forgot it.

But Elizabeth Eleanor Siddal did not forget.

In May of 1852 a very close acquaintance from out of town arrived in London, inquired for Gabriel at Chatham Place, and having been told that he was away from home, went round by Will Little, who coughed and told him that Gabriel, through the kindness of a Miss Barbara Leigh-Smith, was enjoying borrowed quarters in Hampstead Road. William Bell Scott hurried right over there to seek him out.

The evening was at the cool, the cottage dim in the dusk and fragrant with flowering trees. He knocked at the low door but no one answered, which was not surprising since its owner, a cousin of Florence Nightingale's and a strong woman on her own account, was out of town. The breezes stroked the traveler while he considered. There was another little building, half hidden in foliage like a nestling tucked beneath its mother's wing, and though no faint light showed from its tiny windows he knocked there, and waited and then knocked again.

The door flew open.

"Demme!" Gabriel said. "Oh well, you might as well come in."

The lintel was so low that the visitor had to remove his hat, which was just as well, since he saw that there was a lady there, a shadow among shadows, unrelieved by so much as a taper.

Or she was not a lady, since no lady would allow herself to be so compromised — alone, beneath a roof, without lights, with a gentleman? William Bell Scott was a northerner and much excited by London ways; he had a silly little wife at home concerning whom he allowed himself a certain amount of elasticity in conduct, but nothing in his experience indicated to him how, in this instance, manners were to be accommodated. Would there be introductions? He waited and the shadow waited. When no introduction forthcame, he replaced his hat.

The shadow became a willowy girl who brushed by him with her head held high and slipped into the garden. As she moved between dark and dusk he saw her coppery hair, like a sunset's afterglow, and knew it was Miss Siddal.

He could hardly wait to reach Charlotte Street and to tell Christina.

He found the Poet at her tall desk as usual, but instead of her poems she was doing domestic accounts. Maria was home on brief holiday from her governess post at the Reverend Lord Charles Thynne's, but while she usually would have helped with the accounts, she was upstairs uneasily contemplating her future in the household of Lord Charles. It was May, and Mary Month had been trying to her, since she saw signs that her employer, in an excess of enthusiasm, was leaning toward Mariolatry — and indeed soon after that he went over.

Christina smiled for Scott the warm and radiant smile that he, almost alone, could always count on. Her smiles for others were so often derisive, and those for her mother, dim with reverence.

"I have seen her!" he announced. "She exists!"

Christina said, "May we direct ourselves to more pleasant topics?"

Christina was very beautiful, with bright chestnut hair and bright hazel eyes which she too often hid under the heavy lids so like her mother's. Her manners were proper and indeed, almost severe; it would be hard to find a trace of the fiery child she had once been. Yet Christina as a child had been enough to raise a prudent person's hair. One of the "two Storms" rather than the "two Calms" — as the father had lovingly categorized his young — she had been willful, grasping, violent, and rebellious: she had once, in rage at being denied some childish velleity, seized her mother's scissors and with them ripped her arm up its length.

No wonder Frances Lavinia Rossetti worried!

She herself had been a *jeune fille bien élevée* and thoroughly trained to caution and common sense, who in spite of her startling prettiness had committed only one error in her youth, which occurred when she rejected the suit of a Colonel MacGregor, the friend of those who employed her as a governess (she must have been highly thought of to have been allowed downstairs to dine), and accepted that of Gabriele Rossetti, soldier of fortune, rhymester, conspirator, unsound scholar, and, to boot, impoverished. As a result of this choice she had led a long and happy life enriched with love and was determined to prevent her children from making the same mistake.

Maria and William Michael posed no problem. Docile, contented, malleable from the beginning, they were anxious to conform and eager to be instructed; both showed every sign of preserving the norm, although later one joined a nunnery, and, early, the other went bald. They required only a gentle hand and a loose rein. With Gabriel she got nowhere. With Christina, she succeeded beyond what should have been her reasonable expectations. At twenty-two Christina was as coldly controlled, as rigid and as self-abnegating as any careful mother could have wished. She was also often ill.

Now Christina put her pen down carefully, but not without first wiping it. "Gabriel becomes prominent these days," she said dryly. "His paintings hold more promise than his models."

Scott raised the diabolical eyebrows that the ladies found so attractive. They almost met at the centre and at their apex shot off in tufts which, above his steel-coloured eyes, gave him the appearance of that demon lover with whom every young woman would like to match wills. On the other hand, he was much older than she and so was no real danger. Also, he was a man of some property and a poet of sorts; although he had not admitted the existence of his little wife for two long years after he had first crossed the threshold of that fastidious family, he was still accepted as a friend. And in fact he was a man more flirtatious than rapacious, who could be depended upon to retreat at the first threat of victory.

But no young woman, be she ever so austere, is offended by the attentions of an attractive man. And he never overstepped; his eyes spoke, but nothing escaped his lips that was not supportable to her ears. Only within his poems did he refer to her as "Lady-girl."

"Surely," he said, "this girl is more than just another model? Her friends feel that your brother's intentions will prove honest."

She raised her brows in astonishment that Miss Siddal had friends. And then she turned a delicate hand, palm toward him, and he desisted.

"And how," he asked, more securely, "is your papa?"

"Failing, I fear."

Before he left, being a mischievous man, he did refer again to the unwelcome topic.

"One does hear," he said, "that her verses are creditable and her drawings extraordinary. Think, in your charity, what it would mean to her to have the sanction of your acceptance."

After his departure she sat with her hands folded on her lap and feeling, as she always felt when he departed, restless and self-accusatory. This careful pirate who had run up his flag already had forced Christina's frail vessel off its course. It was after she had met William Bell Scott that she had escaped from James Collinson, or he from her, as she would later escape Charles Bagot Cayley. She said it was because of religious differences: Collinson was popish and Cayley, latitudinarian. But William Michael Rossetti thought it was because one was a dunce and the other a priss and that she loved Scott all her life.

She had no right to think of him; it was but fitting that her poems should dwell upon blight, mildew, frost, corruption, and the grave. Though not entirely.

> Because the birthday of my life
> Is come, my love is come to me.

Oh, he was heady company for a sequestered poet! But about one thing he was right: had Christina marshaled her full moral force in favour of the girl, a marriage might have taken place while there was time.

It was too much to ask of woman.

That this unprincipled young woman of no education and no breeding should have left her home and her natural protectors and find, not ignominy, but acclaim! And as a wit, an artist, and a poet! That she moved freely in the world, roamed the fields, sat up of nights in company, and most of all, that the birthday of that girl's life did not go uncelebrated: upon that day her love had stretched his arms, and free and unafraid, she had gone to him.

While she, Christina, older than Lizzie and the better poet, hid in the confines of a shabby home, haunted by ill health: unrecognized, unsought, unpraised, unloved.

And alone with her scruples and her God.

6

ONE THING THAT Lizzie had bargained away in her escape from the Kent Road was the support of the male members of her family. Her father did not require Gabriel to wait upon him, nor did her brother arrive at Chatham Place with a horsewhip. Her self-respect was not endangered, but her respect for Gabriel was, for the first time, in question. For in refusing to acknowledge her to Scott, he betrayed that he was not as indifferent to the opinions of society as he would have her think. She did not think him false, but she began to wonder if he might be weak.

Now no young woman can be comfortable in the thought that she has committed herself to the hands of a weakling, and so it was very natural that she took comfort in the admiration of his friends, some of whom, she thought, understood her better than Gabriel did. Old Brown, for instance.

Ford Madox Brown was called Old Brown because he

was a bit older than the rest of them, married and sober-minded, and suspicious of Gabriel's levity — indeed, they had met when Brown threatened the young genius with a thrashing, having taken his inordinate praise for mockery. Finding he was sincere, Brown gave his devotion to Gabriel and never took it back. To Gabriel's lady, also, he gave his heart.

Old Brown was as bemused by her talents as by her beauty, and he pointed out that her water-colours, though a bit pale and unsure of line, could be mistaken for Gabriel's own. Happily, the deeds of a woman of genius are not judged as severely as the deeds of others.

He also said her poems were very pretty; in his opinion prettier than those of Mrs. Browning, whose *Sonnets from the Portuguese* had recently paved the way for feminine excesses.

Will Little sniffed. "Nobody noticed Mrs. Browning," he said, "before she took off and eloped."

Brown wanted to know what that had to do with anything?

"Furthermore," Will said, "it was Browning with whom she eloped. If she'd been off with the greengrocer no one would have known."

"But she had published before she met Browning."

Ah — but whoever read what she had published?

Browning, for one.

Will Little stopped to calculate. "She must be over forty," he said, shocked.

Those in their first youth are understandably distressed by fierce attachments among the elderly. Suitable loyalty to the partners of their youth is acceptable, but to first form such follies on the very brink of age is grotesque.

Lizzie thought it indelicate that Will should mention such matters in her presence. She blamed him for the course the conversation had taken, irked that it had verged

to Elizabeth Browning from Elizabeth Siddal. She smiled.
Her lambent smile touched one of them and then another,
but it paused when it reached Will and there, briefly, it
glittered.

She moved restlessly. The heavy bell of her full skirts
tugged at her little waist. It seemed to her that she tired
easily these days.

She was not tired of Weymouth Street, nor of the luxury of living alone, nor of the intoxicating knowledge that
she might well be the only irreproachable female in London
to live alone. And she did not tire of not seeing her family,
for she could see them at any time had she been able to
overcome an aversion to their questions and a certain
lassitude that made her unwilling to face the streets and
prefer, when she was not working (for she did call her
water-colours working), to rest in the shabby room that
was so comfortable and to think of the future.

No, what she was tired of was Gabriel's worship of
her, which seemed so far to have little connection with
the future, and of the way he touched her hair and hands
but only her hair and hands, and of the way that he neither
asked nor gave promises.

Because his friends were young and of irreverent habits,
for the most part of no fixed abodes and certainly of no
regular employment, they often went a-Maying, their girls
and baskets on their arms. Once out of London and in
Kew, where there was none to lift an eye except a sheep,
they would separate and couple by couple search seclusion
in the shade — for no improper purposes, of course.

At these times Gabriel, lounging beside Lizzie on the
grass, would loose her hair and play with it, piling it in
shimmering coils or fanning it about her shoulders, and
he would weave circlets of cowslips and primroses and
crown her *Regina Cordium*, the Queen of Hearts. But that
is all he did. If he did no more than that, how was she to

repulse him? If she did not repulse him, how was she to prove herself worthy to be his wife?

And while it is all very well to be a Blessed Damozel, we are told on the best authority that there is no giving and taking in marriage beyond the bar of Heaven, while on this sorry planet no man cleaves long to a woman for her talents, or not as talent is ordinarily understood. Lizzie was fiercely proud that she paid her own rent by means of her own talent, and for proof of the pudding she had offered to her landlord and his lady the professional card that Gabriel had designed for her; neither of them was much impressed.

Will Little explained to her, with some amusement, that models were suspect; indeed, some lessors forbade lessees to paint anything on the premises except still lifes. And he quoted for her the stipulation of the landlord who had once rented 17 Red Lion Square to Walter Deverell. Walter's models, this man had said, "were to be kept under some gentlemanly restraint, as some artists sacrifice the dignity of art to the baseness of passion."

Lizzie had not been much amused.

The landlord had tapped her card nervously in the palm of his hand. He said, "Not in the full figure!"

His wife didn't believe Lizzie was a model at all. Who wanted to paint somebody skinny with red hair? Pretty girls with big hats and cows is what people want.

"Just as long as you don't do it here," she said.

Lizzie's lips tightened, but she kept her temper. Her anger, unfortunately, as it was to prove, was of the kind that turns inward and not out. Many consider this a virtue, and some do not.

On this particular day, annoyed with the talk of Mrs. Browning and even more that Gabriel was off to Charlotte Street, Lizzie met this landlady person in the hall; she bowed formally and went past her, mounting the stairs

with her incandescent head high and cupping her skirts
gracefully at her thigh. But once inside her room she leaned
against the door, feeling her breath tremble in her throat.
And when the water boiled she found, just as she had
thought, that she could not keep down the first sip of tea.
So she removed thankfully from her reticule the small vial
of laudanum that the chemist downstairs had kindly suggested for her nerves.

The chemist was as talkative as he was friendly.

He said, "You know who Paracelsus was? Well, he's
the fellow thought this up — though he told everyone
he made it out of gold and pearls." With the rocklike hand
that chemists have to have he held the vial to eye level and
filled it. "He was a wag, was Paracelsus." He stoppered
the vial tightly. "All it is," he said, "is alcohol and opium.
That's all it is."

If Gabriel were honest with her, he would introduce
her to anyone in the world. If he were loyal to her, he
would not set foot within his parents' house until she had
been asked to enter there.

You were supposed to use three drops in water. A lady
may not partake of spirits, but may use medicine. Elizabeth Siddal tipped the vial above her glass, and the three
oily drops coiled down like snakes.

7

L IZZIE WAS MUCH ALONE; too much, said her friend
Emma Brown.

Young painters, Emma's husband pointed out grimly,
have to paint; whoever is kept waiting, the tradesmen who
supply canvases and stretchers and oils and brushes will
not wait. One day the PRB would all be rich, but in the
meantime buyers were few and far between, and not all
buyers wanted to hang a wraith upon their wall. Some of
them, vulgar though it might be, preferred for daily view-
ing a pinker subject with a bit more bounce.

Emma wanted to know if he was speaking of the Cornforth woman.

For Fanny Cornforth had a lot of bounce and a mass
of soft, heavy, yellow hair.

"Ah, dearest," Old Brown said, "come off of that."

Ford Madox Brown had been widowed young and had
a daughter. His second wife was a warm little woman of
common origin whom Brown himself had educated; he had
waited to see if the education were going to take and it did.

Enough, anyway. The Browns were poor but happy; Emma was useful to her husband, who drew her with her broom, and little Lucy liked her. Unlike some called to high estate, Emma was generous. If she could be so elevated, why not Lizzie?

Brown pointed out that Gabriel could not afford a wife.

"Neither can you!" she said, and threw her warm little housewife's arms about him.

Then she said, "But let them be properly engaged. It would look better."

Ah, this small woman knew her husband's vulnerabilities! Of all the Brotherhood, Brown was the most conventional. Deeply as he was attached to Gabriel, he was often in a fury with him; it was not only that Gabriel cheerfully took his money, such as it was, and did not pay it back, nor that Gabriel would tolerate no one's opinions but his own, nor even that Gabriel confiscated Brown's ideas and used them as his own, but also that his behaviour too often flouted the standards of the very middle class that Brown was struggling to attain. Only last week when he walked with Gabriel, that unregenerate spirit paused in Holborn for two pennyworth of roasted potatoes and ate them in the open. Brown crossed the street and continued on alone.

Of course it would look better if they were engaged. Lizzie was turning difficult of late, but headstrong as she was, her situation would not have come about without Gabriel and in Brown's opinion, a man who sidesteps such responsibility is no gentleman.

It is wonderful what common sense these daughters of the folk demonstrate.

"You are quite right, my love," he told her gloomily. "I don't see what's to be done about it."

"Don't you?" his love said merrily. "I'll think of something."

And besides, Brown was getting a little tired of having

the friend of his friend around the house, where she would flee when she wished to frighten Gabriel, would lie upon the hearth rug looking tragic and would depart leaving behind a household in confusion and ivory bangles, for instance, which Gabriel would demand that Brown return, as if he were trying to make away with them. Nevertheless, Old Brown was Lizzie's friend.

So was John Ruskin.

Ruskin was at that time a youngish man of grim personal probity and great wealth, who had burst early upon a delighted world as a severe judge of art, letters, and architecture. When *Modern Painters* appeared in 1843 an admiring Wordsworth had praised "The Oxford Graduate," and as The Graduate he was known by many from then on.

But John Ruskin was not a happy man. To this fact many of his victims attributed his merciless attacks, which, alas, many listened to with interest and some with glee, as a contributor to *Punch* complained:

> I takes and I paints,
> Hears no complaints
>   And sells before I'm dry;
> Till savage Ruskin
> He sticks his tusk in,
>   Then nobody will buy.

He was, in short, a man who could break as well as make, but to those he admired he showed a generosity and tenderness which, except toward his parents, was nowhere else reflected in his personal life, as his beautiful and rather worldly young wife Euphemia liked to point out. Effie — some called her Effie — may have been somewhat prejudiced; she was a warm and restless girl who, from the first moment when she was alone with her husband, had found her marriage surprising.

"Euphemia," he said, "you understand that to one another we will be as angels."

Well, no, she didn't understand. And being a healthy girl of lively curiosity she had been looking forward to her new estate, which she now found did not suit. At first only surprised, as his angelic abstinence persisted she went through stages of dismay, disdain, and indignation, until she reached a permanent stage of sulks. Gratifying though it may be to have an angel for a husband, most women do look for a little more, and although many a weary woman might have envied her situation, preventing as it did almost all natural responsibilities, Euphemia would have been glad to find out for herself how such responsibilities affected her.

Moreover, and this perhaps was hardest, modesty forbade any mention of such unusual discipline; she could only demean herself by hinting to his parents that she was unwanted and unused, while as long as the old couple remained in ignorance she was demeaned anyway, because she had not produced an heir. Many a stronger woman might have cried "Unfair!"

One would be hard put to isolate the major cause of Ruskin's bitterness, unless it was that he had been allowed no toys except a bunch of keys until the age of three, at which age he was soundly whipped for falling down the stairs. An only child and born late in his parents' lives, he had grown up protected from the world and was educated at home, lest the rough manners of other boys corrupt and perhaps retard the remarkable development of his intelligence; for he was a precocious child who at four had written to an aunt, mildly correcting her for some misheld opinion, and at seven produced an historical work in four volumes.

Wildly encouraged by his parents, he was nonetheless subjected to a Calvinist discipline, and when he went up to Oxford his mother left home for the nonce and accompanied him. His father's ambition was that he win the Newdigate Prize for poetry and so he did; his offering was entitled *Salsette and Elephanta*.

Perhaps it was this very poem that convinced him that he was not really a man of creative gifts; such a discovery has soured the temperament of many a critic. His rich, adorned, and flexible prose style could cajole, threaten, charm, and terrify an adoring public, but the Muse would not draw nigh. Yet the fortune of him whom this great man praised was made — and of him whom he disdained, destroyed.

Because of this, Will Little meant to win his active support for Gabriel Rossetti.

"Mama," he said, "do you know a Mrs. Ruskin?"

Sometimes Mrs. Little felt that her son underestimated her. "I know *the* Mrs. Ruskin," she said pointedly. "Mr. Ruskin is Ruskin of Ruskin, Telford, and Domecq; your father always laid in their wines. I believe they are sinfully rich and cousins of a kind — Mr. and Mrs. Ruskin."

"Could you provide me with an introduction?"

"I could," she said, "but would you wish it? He is in trade."

This did not honestly reflect her son's attitude, nor did she honestly think that it did, but she enjoyed twitting him. Since his papa had died (she missed his papa very much) it sometimes occurred to her unfortunate that Will had not inherited his father's stature and her joie de vivre, instead of the other way about.

And while it was true that the Littles were not in trade and were not sinfully rich, they were very comfortable indeed. Their enviable income was inherited and they had for generations had the good fortune or good sense to produce only one son. Whatever losses had accompanied the dowry of the occasional daughter had been more than recompensed by the foresight of that early Little who had benefited himself as well as his grateful descendants by prudently withdrawing from the South Sea Company the week before the South Sea bubble burst. Since then no Little had accomplished much and none was in the position to look down upon those who had had to earn, if not their bread, at least their petits fours.

"Of course you shall have your letter, dear," she said.

To Will Little's immense relief, when he arrived at Denmark Hill to pay his respects to the bewildered parents of John Ruskin, their distinguished son was present, perhaps to protect them from what must have seemed an unwarranted intrusion.

Ruskin himself was a tall, rusty man in his thirties with bright blue eyes, whose thin mouth was marred. Despite the fact that as a child he had not been allowed to approach water, to run in the fields, nor even to be present at rough games, he had arrived at his own Samarra and as he bent trustfully from the arms of the coachman had been savaged by a black coach dog; the scar twisted his mouth cynically, and many thought him born with a harelip.

The man was suffering, though no one knew it yet. Perhaps he was glad for the distraction of a visitor, particularly one so anxious to enjoy his Turners.

The summer before, Ruskin had taken Johnny Millais, whose strong young talent he much admired, Millais's brother, and Euphemia, and had gone to Scotland, where, in a tiny house in the hamlet of Glenfinlas, they were to invite their souls and Millais was to calm down and paint. It rained day after day; it rained for five weeks. Millais was twenty-four, tall, handsome, and mercurial; Effie was bored and unhappy. The musty, stuffy little house (Millais could touch each wall of his sleeping closet at once and drew a sketch to prove it) drove the men out into the rain, and wherever they went the beautiful little Effie went with them; a brown wide-awake sheltered her hair from the moisture and with woolen plaids she defied the mists.

At the end of five weeks Millais began a portrait of John Ruskin, standing contemplative on rocks as harsh as his jaw, in a frock coat, before a rushing stream. By this time the warm, young Johnny had noticed that the husband was cold and the young wife miserable. It is certain that in some quiet spot, sheltered beneath a tree or in the shallow cave provided by some crag, she confided in him, though perhaps not the fact that her husband had been unpleasantly surprised to find that women are not as unfurred as are statues. He had been offended.

The winter that followed that foray into Scotland was wretched for everyone, and in April Effie, accompanied by Ruskin's valet, saw Ruskin off on the railway train upon some business of his own. At the last minute, from the window of the train he tossed a purse of money to her, in a way that she, at least, thought contemptuous.

"There is nothing any longer you can do to prevent me," she called up, and flung it back at him.

Then she went home, packed her things, and left for her parents at Perth.

John Ruskin was an odd man, but a good one. Informed, prejudiced, and violently fair, it did not occur to him that the portrait should not be finished. But he suffered. A gentleman is not abandoned by his wife: it exposes him to the chatter of his inferiors.

"My dear sir," Will said, "your generosity is as well known as your perspicacity. When these young men were sore beset you were the first to lend the weight of your name to their defense."

Ruskin nodded. The young man, of course, referred to those letters in *The Times*.

Will cleared his throat deferentially and quoted. " 'There

has been nothing in art so earnest or so complete,' " he said,
" 'since the days of Albrecht Dürer.' "

Well, Ruskin had been angry with those so lulled by
dark, shiny brown landscapes that they were appalled by
J. M. W. Turner's world that dissolved in light, smoke,
and mist, and he was in a mood to stand up for the new.
But it is pleasing when someone recalls your very words.

"And then," Will said, "your lectures in Edinburgh."

"I will show you something," Ruskin said.

He led the way upstairs to his own rooms where from
an immaculately ordered cabinet he withdrew a drawing
which an excited Will recognized as Gabriel's. It was
Dante Drawing an Angel in Memory of Beatrice and was
hotly admired by Gabriel's defenders.

"This was sent me by a man who purchased it," Ruskin
said. "He wishes my opinion of its worth."

The man was MacCracken, an Irishman acute in business and unsure in art; Will knew that and that Gabriel
hoped it would be one of many such sales.

"It is exquisite," Ruskin said. "I shall tell Mr. Mac-
Cracken so."

This was Will's opening. "But it does little good," he
said, carefully exercising his own art, "to praise the artist
if the man must starve."

8

THIS WAS ADROIT of Will, knowing as he did that Ruskin believed the possession of wealth to be a grave responsibility. It was not quite honest, since his friend was in no immediate danger of starvation. When Gabriel could not pay the rent, his brother could; if he was hungry he could go home; if he needed colours Lizzie usually had a shilling or two; and if he thirsted for diversion he invited in his friends, with the request that they bring the oranges and wine. No, he was in no real discomfort, although like any sensible man he would have preferred to frequent better eatinghouses, to travel, to possess the silks and brocades and the gold in which he dressed his models and which must, alas, be returned eventually to those from whom they had been borrowed.

But he was not sure that he wished to be secure enough to marry. Lizzie adorned his pictures but was no good to him in bed nor in his moments of boisterous merrymaking. You could not slap Lizzie's rump.

But it was no part of Will Little's plan that Gabriel should marry Lizzie, who Will felt had forfeited by her bizarre behaviour any claim to the dignity of wife. Besides, in four years she had thinned and paled. In fact, Ford Madox Brown had written in his diary — never mind how Will knew; he was capable of stooping in the name of friendship — "Saw Miss Siddal, looking thinner and more beautiful and more ragged than ever."

More beautiful? But then Brown and his wife had ever been Lizzie's friends.

Moreover, Will suspected (and thought the Browns did, too) that many an evening when Gabriel made no account of himself he spent with Fanny Cornforth, who was not at the moment living with her spouse. No, no, one does not marry models, and when Gabriel became rich, Guggums — for such was Gabriel's ridiculous name for her (she called him Gug) — could be pensioned off.

But he had not counted on the exquisite sensibilities of John Ruskin.

For Ruskin wrote not only to MacCracken but to Gabriel himself, who wrote in turn and in great glee to Ford Madox Brown.

"MacCracken sent my drawing to Ruskin," he exulted, "who the other day wrote me an incredible letter about it, remaining mine respectfully (!!), and wanting to call. I of course stroked him down in my answer and yesterday he called. . . . He seems in a mood to make my fortune."

They had been quarreling just before Ruskin knocked at the door of Chatham Place. They had been quarreling over Annie Miller.

Annie had been discovered by Holman Hunt, who was given to large canvases that told little stories highly moral in their message. Annie sat for *The Awakened Conscience*, in which, struck by a chord of music that brings back the cot of her parents, the model recoils from the cad who has surrounded her with elaborate furniture and easier ways. The chord of music is struck by a caged bird. Gabriel liked the subject and he liked the girl, who was a romp and a flirt.

He began his own picture and called it *Found;* he purposed a country girl cowering beside a meticulously painted brick wall and discovered by the bumpkin who had loved her in the days when she was pure. The lout was to be taking a calf to market — the Brotherhood was fond of animals. He had bullied a reluctant Hunt into letting Annie sit for the country girl.

Holy Hunt was reluctant because he was so taken with Annie that, encouraged by Brown's example, he had hoped to teach her table manners and to make her his wife; perhaps he did not totally trust his friend. Then too, Annie was no Emma Brown, but liked to kick her heels and share a mug of ale, and she grew restive under Hunt's instruction.

"If you have no concern for me," Lizzie said hotly, "you might consider the feelings of your friend."

"But how have I offended either?"

All he had done was to squire Annie about a bit in Holman Hunt's absence, though he had signed a paper for Hunt saying that he would not do that. Torn between alternatives, Hunt had followed his art instead of his heart and was off to the Holy Lands, the better to observe an actual goat upon the actual barren sands. *The Scapegoat*, with the phylactery about its neck, made his name but cost him Annie, who had decided that Gabriel Rossetti was more fun.

However, there had been no real harm in it. By nightfall Lizzie was too tired to wish to do more than to sit in the dusk; she lost her breath when she tried to dance, and the heat and noise of the music halls made her head ache. Gabriel had taken Annie to Madame Tussaud's and to dance in Piccadilly, and once or twice he had brought her back to Chatham Place. But there was no way that Lizzie could know that.

He looked impatiently at her. She was almost as beautiful as she had been when he first saw her, but not quite. The bright colour in her cheeks was subdued and she was frail, not merely fragile; she had been slender as a green flower stalk and now grew brittle. Only her hair still burned and glowed.

She knew that his cool artist's eyes evaluated her and her own eyes grew hot under their long white lids; she dropped them to the drawing in her lap. Oh, she resented Annie Miller and Fanny Cornforth, too, and all the light loves in the life of her intended, but she had not been brought up in the small house of a large family for nothing, and she knew that as long as she would not give herself to him, he would not wait for her. Some things, in reason, must be overlooked.

But in bringing Annie to Chatham Place he had committed an error Lizzie was to find hard to forgive: any one of his friends might have knocked and sought the key beneath the mat, and finding no response and no entry might very well have decided that he had a woman there and that the woman was Elizabeth Siddal. What else were they to think?

How had she known? Oh, women always know. Rivals, through rage or mischief, always leave some sign; some small, inexplicable, and foreign object, or a familiar one impudently disarranged.

The look in Gabriel's sultry face would not give itself a name; perhaps it was anger. At any rate, when Ruskin knocked at the door the charcoal snapped in Gabriel's hand. But when he saw who stood there, hesitant, he changed as quickly as light on shot silk and all his colours sparkled and grew bright.

At thirty-five, Ruskin was not a handsome man, although he was by no means as ugly as he thought. As a painter, Gabriel regretted Ruskin's narrow face; with his neat hair and rusty colour he would make a poor angel and a dull knight. But the man was in pain, and pain is interesting.

Careless Gabriel might be and unfaithful, an opportunist perhaps; he was not without sympathy. It was Gabriel's opinion that Johnny Millais was an ass. If the woman hared off from her husband, what was that to Millais? She could do Johnny's art no good but only saddle him with care. And if all he heard about John Ruskin was true — it seemed it was — the man should not have been let out without his nurse. But he was honestly sorry for any man of gifts who could not manage a mere woman, and it was with no mockery that he bowed to his guest.

"Honoured," he said.

Like many a shy man, Ruskin had a way of veering sharply between self-effacement and arrogance. He entered, looked for a place to place his hat, cane, and gloves, and finding every surface covered, elected to retain them. Then he returned the bow coldly, and seeing the young woman topped with flame and dressed in billowy grey, he waited to be introduced.

Lizzie waited, too.

She had not forgotten and would never overlook that Gabriel had refused her in the presence of William Bell Scott, whom she now, of course, hated. She had been pleased to see that Scott had not, artistically, prospered; his cumbersome poetical efforts were largely ignored except by the intimate and curious who knew that although his *Mignon* poems had been for Christina, he had since attached himself to a wealthy Alice Boyd and to a Lady Trevelyan, all of whom scamped along together in curious accord, while Christina sulked and suffered.

But Christina's false suitor was one thing; John Ruskin

was another. He was a visitor from the World, a man of dignity and substance and acclaim, before whom Elizabeth Siddal must be justified.

And Gabriel, who should have named her as his future wife, said only, "This is Miss Siddal."

John Ruskin saw her shudder and avert her face. He recognized another fine spirit brutally misused; but still, the man had talent.

"May I see?" Ruskin asked, and without permission he took the drawing from her lap.

Lizzie's drawing was weak and her chiaroscuro improbable, but the drawing had a kind of nervous power, not altogether agreeable, that riveted his attention. Two pairs of lovers met and drew back in horror to see their doppelgänger. Later, Gabriel would seize the idea as his own and would call it *How They Met Themselves*.

But now, John Ruskin gently replaced the drawing upon her knees.

"Remarkable," he said. "I hope there are others?"

Silently she arose and brought him her portfolio while Gabriel, patient and amused, attended. Ruskin leafed through her lovers and ladies; his fine hands, delicate and tender, moved quickly but his searching eyes missed nothing.

"You are greatly gifted," he heard himself say.

And then to Gabriel, "Well, well, turn them over, let's have a look."

Gabriel kept his canvases face to the wall because of dust and because he did not easily invite the opinion of fools. But this man was no fool and could be useful. He held his peace while Ruskin moved slowly from one to another: they glowed, they shone, the ambers and the golds, the scarlets and purples exploded in the shabby room.

At last Ruskin, pointing with his cane, announced of

one, "Please put a dab of Chinese white into the hole in the cheek and paint it over."

He thought for a moment and then added, "Never put raw green into light flesh."

Gabriel held his tongue. Already he was framing in his mind a line to his friend the sculptor Thomas Woolner. "As he is only half informed about Art," he would say, "anything he says in favour of one's work is of course sure to prove invaluable in a professional way."

And now Ruskin, separating the chaff from the wheat, nudged away with his cane a canvas he did not like, and having hesitated over one he did like, said, "Try to get it a little less like worsted-work by Wednesday, when I will send for it."

Gabriel did not mind that the wine merchant's son spoke in this way, since Ruskin had the ear of every editor in the country and his finger on the cheque-book of more than one collector with more money than experience. Because, in Gabriel's opinion, wealth exists for art and more particularly for the artist, this dried husk of an unhappy man, ten years his senior, might be excused some small offenses. Besides, in more than one way, he might be put to use. Gabriel looked thoughtfully at Lizzie.

Before he left, Ruskin bowed deeply over her thin hand with its blue nails and said to Gabriel Rossetti, "She is a glorious creature."

Lizzie shot Gabriel a look of triumph.

Who knows why?

Did Ruskin wish to compensate Elizabeth Siddal for the fame he meant to win for Gabriel? Or was he moved to ruth by one, like himself, rejected? Or did he wish to prove to others and perhaps to himself, that he was vulnerable to female charms?

All that is certain is that the next month in the Ecclesiastical Courts, Euphemia Grey, "falsely known as Ruskin," sued Ruskin for divorce on the grounds of impotence. Then in her father's house and by the same Scottish rites which had solemnized the fiasco of her first union, she married John Everett Millais. That young man wept all through their wedding trip and had to be comforted by his bride; as if he were a frightened child, she held him to her bosom.

As might have been expected, Ruskin was cut on the street by all decent people, but he did not allow that to interfere with the completion of his portrait. There he stands on the rocks and lichens, hat in hand, his starched collar rubbing his narrow jaw, his frock coat flawless, while behind him the torrent boils.

For as he said, "It would be better that she were broken on the wheel than come between me and John Millais!"

9

GABRIEL, IN A RAGE, paced the small balcony at Chatham Place.

"It's not my fault," Will Little said plaintively, from within.

He had not followed his friend out upon the balcony for a number of reasons. He didn't trust the balcony; the fact that it looked sturdy didn't prove it was. Also, it was small, and Gabriel was too restive to insure that his paint-wet clothing would not brush against Will's coattails.

"I was only defending you," Will said.

Gabriel paused and glared. Spare him such defense! Of course it was Will's fault, but to be fair, not entirely. Emma Brown was much to blame and Lizzie herself, if only because she was not robust; had she not been ill, none of these sorry circumstances would have occurred.

Gabriel pressed his stained fingers to his forehead, as if to hold in place the vein that was beginning to throb there. He might be going to have another headache. Lizzie was not the only one who was not robust.

Oh, the ills from which they all suffered!

It was a suffering century; little was known of many ailments save their symptoms, and many of the nostrums to which they resorted were curious and deadly. Lock of the bowel was comforted by applying heat; then the appendix burst. Though cholera occurred and typhoid fever was a constant fear, no one seemed to associate either with sluggish drains or none at all. One bled for fevers; every apothecary kept leeches to facilitate the bleeding.

There was also brain fever, which, particularly among the ladies, was pandemic. Perhaps that was because the term covered a multiplicity of troubles. Brain fever might be caused by tumors, by encephalitis, by mental disorder, by the megrims (a term applied in its turn to migraines), by melancholia and hypochondria, all of which spring from bottled anger.

The Brotherhood, one and all, had excruciating headaches which were in a way a tribute to their art, since in rejecting the muddy canvases which their predecessors considered rich and seemly, they whitened theirs with lead paint; their persistent breathing of the fumes did not prove wholesome. At Chatham Place the fetid air threatened fever, and although they overcame that danger by burning herbs, as Lizzie's health worsened those consulted forbade her Chatham Place — but she preferred to worsen.

Like myriad others, Effie Millais had sustained painful quinsy sore throats that seemed to settle in her tonsils, but since when tonsils were removed the patient bled to death, chloroform was prescribed to alleviate the discomfort. From his own debilitating sore throats, John Ruskin thought he found relief in massage, which was called shampoo. Effie was also a martyr to a tic douloureux, the spasms of which were painfully visible — but that was before she fell in love. Three of Effie's little sisters had died within weeks of one another of scarlet fever; naturally when later Sophie and Alice, John, Melville, Albert, and George had the scarlet fever, everyone was troubled and Effie, who at the time had needed badly to retreat to her family, was not permitted to do so.

People had long suspected that The Sid suffered from consumption; that was a natural conclusion — so many did. In the case of such gradual wasting, nobody thought to isolate the sick from the well, and since the night air is dangerous, one took no chances with the air at all, but kept the patient's room hot, close, and swathed with cloth. Ruskin himself as a young man had spat blood but was saved by a physician of advanced opinions who put him on a diet of saltwater and hard bread.

It is more than possible that Lizzie could have facilitated the diagnoses of her doctors had she been willing to admit dyspepsia, but she was not. An upset stomach will not hold a reluctant lover, however much his whims and failures may have contributed to it. Pallor, loss of weight, and fainting spells, especially alternating with hysteria, can more quickly bring a recalcitrant man to his knees.

Gabriel was not irresponsible in all ways. He didn't even — at that time — have any vices. He was selfish to the bone and easily bored, but he was not unkind. It was certainly no part of his plan, if he could be said to have a plan, to ruin any young woman, and he was honestly alarmed when his friends pointed out that, in their estimation, Lizzie was in decline.

Then he gnawed his stained thumb and spat. The pigment tasted no better than it ever did.

In his alarm he had turned to the same young friend who had made available to him the very studio in which he had not introduced Lizzie to Scott. Barbara Leigh-Smith was a jolly, wealthy young woman and a good fellow, who thought nothing of hiking her skirts up to her plump thighs in order to scramble through a brook. It was her first suggestion that Lizzie should retire to the Hos-

pital for Diseased Gentlewomen, in the founding of which
her cousin Miss Florence Nightingale had been instru-
mental. This Lizzie vigorously declined to do. But then,
through Barbara's offices and with the help of her purse,
lodgings were found for Lizzie at the seashore, where she
agreed to retreat for a time. Gabriel had said that he would
accompany her to see that she traveled safely and would
stay for a few days to see her comfortably settled in.

Emma Brown had been gratified. For a gentleman to
travel with a lady and to remain under the same roof in
public lodgings — was this not tantamount to a declara-
tion?

Not in Gabriel's understanding.

Number 5 High Street, Hastings, was a strange little
house with one room upstairs and one down, very old and
so dilapidated that the adjoining houses seemed to be
leaning to hold it up. The house was chill and damp, the
weather wet and windy; the strand was deserted and the
small fire smoked. Underneath there were divers passages
and closets, said to have been used by smugglers and now
to be haunted; a queer place, altogether, to expect a lonely
and troubled girl to amuse herself. Gabriel had hurried
right back to London, feeling virtuous and relieved.

Lizzie would not have stayed there long in any event,
even had it not been for Will Little and Emma Brown.

But Emma and Will had words.

Brown was away, so Will would not have been at the
Browns' at all that day except that Gabriel, as a particular
favour, had asked him to pick up a certain shawl that
Brown possessed and that Gabriel wanted. He needed that
shawl. And although he didn't intend to paint it until
tomorrow, he wanted Will to get it today because Brown
was not going to be at home to prevent his getting it. Will
pointed out that Emma was fierce as a lioness in defense
of her husband's interests, and Gabriel replied that that

was the beauty of it. Had he been after something sumptuous she wouldn't let him have it, but she wouldn't know how important the old shawl was in which Brown liked to draw her sweeping. But Brown would know. And how was Gabriel to paint darns and thin spots unless he had darns and spots to observe?

Oh, very well.

Unfortunately, the conversation turned to Lizzie.

"Not at all," Will said, bristling. "No such thing. Nothing of the sort. If anything in the way of an engagement existed, I would be first to know."

Emma Brown pursed her pink lips and smoothed her skirts upon her knees. What he had said implied not only that Dante Gabriel Rossetti had no intention of marrying her friend, but that if he had had such an intention she, Emma Brown, would not be the first to know. His friendship was thus exalted and hers, impugned.

It was because of this that she said, "Little do you know."

Something about that innocent phrase raises a disproportionate ire in the hearer.

"In the case of an engagement," Will said, "surely it would have been announced?"

And he smiled blandly, implying that such an announcement could work only to Lizzie's good.

Oh, indeed?

"Her family is very old and proud," Emma said.

"So I have heard her say."

"They dislike his profession, and are much opposed to the match."

Since this implied that the shopgirl came from a family empowered to look down upon scholars and patriots, Will Little looked very hard at Emma Brown.

Emma was a good woman, and a dear young woman, and a loving and loyal friend, but she was simple — not stupid, but uncomplicated — and could in no way com-

prehend that the complicated Lizzie cringed to be spoken
of or even to be thought about. That her supporters should
consider her situation and defend it was to concede that
her situation was delicate, and would have made her feel
as exposed as if she were discovered in her stays.

To be the subject of tea talk! To have the sympathy
that recognized that she required sympathy! And of all
people, to have Barbara Leigh-Smith, whose sturdy goodwill much exceeded her tact, called upon for the defense of
Elizabeth Siddal!

But in her innocence Emma said to Will Little, "Do you
for one moment think that Miss Leigh-Smith, unless she
were privy to the facts, would countenance, let alone assist,
any irregularity?"

Will Little went right home and penned a protest to
Miss Leigh-Smith on behalf of his gifted friend who could
not, would not, should not assume responsibility for an
erratic young woman who, however talented, seemed to
lack any sense of what was seemly. Of the goodness of his
heart, Dante Gabriel Rossetti had become encumbered, and
should not be embarrassed by any further claim than that
made upon a generous spirit by a young person in need of
generosity.

But Miss Leigh-Smith, that jolly fellow, on the whole
approved of women more than she did of men and was
bright enough to be cognizant of how much her own bank
account contributed to her own independence. She had
gathered about her a little cluster of like-minded women
who refused to admit that they were Adam's ribs and
didn't give a toot for the notion that marriage alone con-
ferred respectability. She was much offended by Will
Little's letter, which seemed to make of her the kind of
person who gave a toot.

So sitting at her desk, she took her pen in hand. Then
she spoke to her Roman Catholic friend who was choosing
for her bedchamber an appropriate icon. But should it be

Saint Agnes? Saint Catherine? Saint Theresa? And if Saint
Theresa, which Theresa?

"Hush," Barbara said, and shook the ink from her steel
quill.

She hooked a lock of pretty, unkempt hair behind her
ear, and then she wrote to Gabriel Rossetti. She said that
it had come to her attention. She said that she herself didn't
give a toot. She said (and here the quill dug into the
paper) that she had the greatest sympathy for anyone who
was the subject of the discourse of simpletons. She said
that unless he could see his way clear to protecting a most
unusual individual from the gossip of dunces, he need not
expect her further assistance now, or at any other time.

"Now," she said to her friend. "How about Theresa of
Avila? You can get her in pink."

When Lizzie received Gabriel's hot and reproachful
letter that accused her of playing upon the sympathies of
Emma Brown she had hysterics, developed violent stomach
pains, withdrew to her couch, and refused nourishment.
Daily she dwindled.

The landlady, a Mrs. Elphick, plunged into the correspondence; she thought — indeed, she really thought —
that Mr. Rossetti had better come, and quickly, too. Gabriel was terrified at what he had possibly done. To do him
credit, he didn't care much about the money because there
were a lot of places where he could get some money and
he didn't seem to need all that much of it. He had no time
to marry while his career was quickening, but there must
be something he could do to help Lizzie short of marriage.
A proud man himself, he did understand that she was
rubbed raw by all of this unwelcome attention.

It must be said in his defense that she had led him to
believe that she was free as a bird, which was an unfortunate comparison, since Gabriel hated birds. They were
too light, too hollow, they beat and panicked, and they

had hard little tightening, horny, scrabbling claws. A bird must be decorative indeed to attract Gabriel.

Fanny Cornforth had never mastered Gabriel's name.

"Rizzetty," this plump, kind, and accommodating model said, "I don't see why you got to go."

One of the nice things about Fanny Cornforth was that one didn't have to test for ulterior opinions; once she had said she didn't understand, she had made her position clear: she simply didn't understand.

By now he was stuffing clothing frantically into his portmanteau, but he paused to slap her affectionately on her flowered bottom. "You're an untidy slut," he told her fondly.

She said, "I can't just wait around for you. I can get five bob tomorrow somewheres else."

He said, "You do that. But when I'm ready, Fan, I want you back."

"Oh," she said, "I'll be back."

Gabriel took a diligence, but first he had to take the railway train, although he was still afraid of it — like many another. Mrs. Ruskin, for one, trembled and wept each time her famous son entrusted himself to the iron horse. And yet he survived safely every trip except that one, which he had not discussed with his mother. No tunnel, no drunken engineer, no vengeful porter could have been as lethal to John Ruskin as the little purse that his wife had flung back across his face.

And yet Euphemia Grey and John Everett Millais were happy ever after. He became Sir John Millais and immensely popular; perhaps retribution should have overtaken them, but what happened was that Effie and Johnny grew rich and attractive, and she bore him a bevy of happy children. Perhaps once in a while they were troubled.

But they slept warm.

Meantime, Lizzie's cheeks were apricot with anger; she waited for her lover in a passion of resentment that brought the blood pounding in her wrists and rising to her cheeks in a way that imitated health — her very hair seemed to spark.

They had become as inimical to one another, these sweethearts, as if they were already wed. Perhaps their attraction had always been unsound: what she sought in Gabriel was a wider world than that offered by the Kent Road; what he felt for her was the desire to possess and be gratified (both she refused him). Their pleasure in one another — she in his promise, he in her beauty — was gone, though each pretended it was not. Their tug-of-war was still the same: she would marry and he would not. Or call it warfare: each employed the same weapon — she used her failing health to compel him and he used it to escape her proud and accusatory presence.

Lizzie had given this much thought.

So she waited until she heard the knocker bark sharply against the thin door that opened on the crooked, cobbled street, until she heard the clatter of Mrs. Elphick's boots, the muted rumble of Gabriel's voice and his quick light steps upon the narrow stairs, and then she took a deep, quivering breath and changed utterly. She stretched her hands to him, her smile glittered, her hair burned in the shabby, shadowy room.

"Gug, darling," she said warmly.

And arrested by her unexpected welcome and by the energy that blazed through her thin body, he kissed the corner of her mouth and then, feeling the welcome of her long legs under their heavy skirt against his, his arms went about her and he kissed the sweet mouth with its short upper lip again, and at length.

For Emma Brown had told Lizzie that in her absence, Fanny Cornforth played chatelaine at Chatham Place.

10

A ND NOW A WONDERFUL thing happened for Elizabeth Siddal.

John Ruskin was very pleased at the betrothal of his
protégés; perhaps he took more credit for it than the facts
warranted. He had moved back with his parents at Denmark Hill, and there he wished to entertain at tea the
affianced couple.

The old people were ecstatic to have their son safely
home; they had missed his company and had never trusted
Euphemia to see that he dressed suitably for the weather
or that he ate correctly, and it was even the old gentleman's belief that Effie had padded her domestic accounts
in order to wring money from her husband. But still, the
Ruskins did not entertain. As was their wont, they did not
discuss it until John Ruskin left the room.

"Oh, I think not," Mrs. Ruskin said then. "What a
notion."

"I hardly think, my love, we can refuse."

"But Mr. Ruskin! Think on it! The young man is an intimate friend of . . . of . . ." And she faltered, unable to bring herself to utter the abhorred name of John Millais.

"Nevertheless," said Mr. Ruskin.

"And the young woman? Is she received by his parents? Because I cannot think it proper of us to encourage a liaison of which his family does not approve."

Mr. Ruskin explained that she would now be received and that if she had not been so as yet it could only be because the engagement was very new and old Mr. Rossetti very ill. John had said so.

Very well, then. If John had said so.

But those young people should not discover the likeness of that woman enshrined in the house of Ruskin. One and all, the Ruskins revered art, and Mrs. Ruskin was no less reverent than the gentlemen. But before she penned a note to Miss Siddal, the outraged mother placed over the marble bust of Euphemia Grey a large antimacassar.

Just as her friend John Ruskin had expected, Lizzie's wounded sensibility was somewhat assuaged by the invitation to Denmark Hill. She had thought that more would change with her engagement than had changed; Gabriel still visited Charlotte Street alone, and every time he went there she felt as if a hand clutched her entrails. Perhaps if, as she had wished, their intentions had been published in *The Times*?

But Gabriel would not. Not, he said, until a day could be set for the wedding; he could not, at the moment, foresee when that would be. Reluctantly, she agreed that such publishment would raise expectations in both the well-wishing and the malicious, and what could she tell them as the weeks, perhaps even the months, went by? They would begin to whisper that she might yet be jilted.

But jealous of her new position, she was anxious about how she would be treated by the elder Ruskins: would they accord her her due? Because if they did not, someone must be held to account. Dressing in her room at Weymouth Street, she raised her head with its massy weight of red-gold and listened balefully, while next door her affianced paced impatiently.

Her glass gave back a handsome figure in a black and gold striped gown that did not much resemble the kind of frock in which a young girl would appear at tea. Well, she was not a young girl. She was over twenty, an independent woman and herself an artist; Ruskin himself had said so. More and more it was becoming vital to her that her gifts be recognized, since in the name of genius even a woman may walk alone without inviting contumely. Others had done it: there was George Sand (though Lizzie herself would perish before she would appear in trousers); there was George Eliot, who lived openly with George Henry Lewes; there was Rosa Bonheur (though no one could reasonably object to the horses that she painted). Mademoiselle Bonheur had been first a dressmaker, as Lizzie had made bonnets.

Gabriel called, "Guggums! Are you ready?"

One thing she could not afford to do was to embarrass him by becoming faint or ill. She measured out the laudanum that she had come to depend on and looked longingly at the brandy which made the drops so much more palatable. But that, today, would not do.

Denmark Hill was the largest single dwelling that Lizzie had ever entered, and she suspected that the same was true of Gabriel, but he was not intimidated. Lizzie was. A barracks of a place, it was set sternly in undecorated grounds. Had the Ruskins been taken with that odd enthusiasm they could well have afforded topiary, but they were not interested even in natural shrubs. The broad, flat lawns were severely disciplined, the outbuild-

ings neat and sturdy (the estate had originally been a
farm), but nothing suggested that the owners had even
a cursory care for the out-of-doors.

Within, the chairs and ottomans were huge and hard,
the tables innocent of throws, and the big, square rooms
resembled nothing so much as a museum. The halls, the
walls, were hung with drawings, etchings, paintings, mez-
zotints, which the father had first bought because the son
persuaded him that they were good investments, and then
because he had learned to cherish them. Foremost among
them was a Tintoretto. And then the Turners that smoked
and blazed and were all gathered now beneath the paternal
roof; for these the son had traded much of the income
that Effie had been blamed for squandering.

Lizzie bowed, wary and graceful in her golden stripes.

Mr. Ruskin was shorter than she had pictured him,
with a dandelion shock of white hair and a round little
belly; Mrs. Ruskin was far grander; both were warm and
welcoming. Lizzie was not taken in: they were gentlefolk.
But she was pleased not only to be escorted upstairs to see
other treasures but to have her opinion of them solicited.
This was a graceful recognition of her difference; John
Ruskin, then, had repeated at home the praise he had
offered her at Chatham Place. When they returned to the
withdrawing room she was more at ease and more inclined
to trust in their goodwill. This trust became her.

Lizzie knew herself to be adept with a teacup and she
felt appreciated; the light was gathering in her agate eyes
and the rose rising gently in her cheeks and the little tea
party might have contributed greatly to her sense of worth.

But alas, it was not to be.

For they were interrupted at this point by a maid as
spare and proud as her mistress. A hansom cab waited at
the door and Mr. Rossetti was required at home. His father
would not last the day.

Gabriel's sudden confusion told Elizabeth Siddal that he had known all along of this dire possibility, for otherwise William Michael would not have known where to send for him. But he had not mentioned it to her, although, as his affianced wife, she should have been included in this crisis at Charlotte Street; that she was not meant those at Charlotte Street did not know she was his affianced wife.

As the enormity of his betrayal became clear to her she half rose and subsided weakly with her golden head thrown against the sofa back. Mrs. Ruskin was at her side at once to chafe her cold and narrow wrists.

"I am sorry, I am so sorry," Lizzie murmured faintly.

Old Mr. Ruskin felt that such distress over a parent was wholly admirable.

"Not at all," he said fiercely. "It does you honour."

Gabriel already had his coat and gloves. Lizzie attempted to rise, though unsteadily.

He said, "But I must go alone."

"Of course," she answered, willing her voice to gentleness.

And in any case, the Ruskins would not hear of it. She was too vulnerable for such an ordeal; no, he must go at once and she must stay. Their coachman should see her safely back to Weymouth Street and John Ruskin himself would accompany her.

Why, she had not yet even had her tea!

So the old patriot was dying, he who had known Mazzini, whose impassioned lyrics had helped to inflame Italy. He lay propped against tall pillows with them all around him — his sons, his daughters, his beloved wife. It had been some time since he could distinguish them by sight but he didn't need to — he knew the whisper of their skirts and could tell the cool loving son from the warm loving one. He would know throughout eternity the touch of one. He would know throughout eternity the touch of Frances Lavinia's hand. He lay content enough and in no pain, and if he did not babble of green fields, it was not because they were not there to babble of.

Oh, he had had a glorious youth! Had heard the populace acclaim him, had had a child by an illicit love he might have married had he not had to fly from his enemies disguised — through the assistance of a noble woman — as a woman. And lo! In a strange land he had made his way and by his tempestuous wooing had won this paragon for his wife. He had been feared as a man should be feared, and loved as a man should be loved.

About him his family waited, fairly patiently. This is not to cavil with them; their grief was no less real because the chairs were hard and the hours long, because a nose tickled or a limb cramped; nature is clever at leading her children into loss; such small discomforts relieve those about to be bereaved from the enormity of what is happening, and William Michael cannot be held to account that he sighed, ever so slightly. With the paterfamilias gone, he would become responsible for them all.

Beside him the black beads of Maria's rosary ticked and Christina gave her an impatient glance, since the small sound distracted her from the contemplation every Christian soul should invite when in the presence of the Angel. And in fact so moved was she by her father's final predicament that her poet's heart was moved to silent song.

> When I am dead, my dearest,
> Sing no sad songs for me . . .

Oh, sad, sad! And she still in her youth!

> Plant thou no roses at my head,
> Nor shady cypress-tree: . . .

She touched her eyes delicately with her handkerchief.

At the moment the old man's thoughts wandered far from them all. It seemed impossible that it should all be over, so soon, so soon, when it was all as close as yesterday, the hot blood rushing in the manly veins, the towering intellect, the siring of sons. That he should have to steal away so meekly, who had shaken thrones!

Gabriel suddenly bent his dark curls down upon his father's wasted knees. He wept.

Old Gabriele stirred restlessly. Frances Lavinia, her lined face serene, touched her son's shoulder reprovingly and thought of the task that lay ahead. Before the day was out she must burn her husband's manuscripts, every last one of them. They were blasphemous.

And now he touched one hand with the other wonderingly, so thin and knotted and enfeebled had it become. He had been much blessed, but it is a rude guest who overstays his time. No, no, enough. Enough. Just as he had as a young man felt a natural impatience with restraint of any kind, the old man tired now of the way they were all closing in upon him with the burden of their reverence. He had done all he could for them and was leaving for them a glorious heritage; upon the rolls of honour, the name of Gabriele Rossetti would stand forever with that of Dante Alighieri.

Almost in petulance, he turned his blinded eyes aside. He loved them, he would always love them. But he could do no more.

And in another moment, he slipped away to green fields.

11

AND IN FACT, the Ruskins had taken quite a fancy
to Elizabeth Siddal. Mrs. Ruskin said that while it
was plain that she was of pathetically uncertain health —
Gabriel must take great care of her — it was equally apparent that her manners, her carriage, and her sensibility
were all beyond reproach. Perhaps she had always wished
to have a daughter.

Mr. Ruskin, carried away, cried out, "Why, she could
be a countess!"

Their son said nothing. But John Ruskin was a tender
man and his own judgment was often influenced by his
enthusiasm. He was touched by Lizzie's situation and
honestly believed her to be the possessor of unusual talents; at the same time he knew Gabriel to be the real
genius and was eager for his success. He wanted to see
them marry, and that, as soon as it was feasible; but in
the meantime he knew that anything that lessened Lizzie's

need would contribute to Gabriel's time and temper. He
gave all this much thought.

And the next time John Ruskin called at Chatham
Place, he came with peculiar gifts. For Lizzie, from his
father, he brought an opal which, however, he delivered
to Gabriel; in view of the fact that the superstitious believe that gem to be unlucky, he feared the effect of its
connotations upon an excited mind. From his mother he
brought a small quantity of ivory dust ground from the
tusks of elephants — this to be boiled with herbs. The re-
sultant jelly was strengthening and known to be a positive
specific against the consumption.

Then to Elizabeth Siddal he offered a gift of his own.

"My dear girl," he said, "you have very great abilities."

Lizzie flushed with pleasure. He had not added "for a
woman," and she had not so understood him.

"However," he continued, "your strength is limited and
your powers must be conserved."

She did not wish Gabriel to think otherwise.

"Therefore," he said, "I should like to drive a bargain
with you." And he looked at her very hard.

He would purchase from her all drawings or paintings
she could produce and would pay her, for the privilege,
an income of one hundred and fifty pounds annually. Or,
if she preferred, he would act as her agent, and she should
receive the full purchase price of all that he could sell.
However . . . and again he looked very hard at her.

"You must first agree to place yourself for a time in
the hands of a physician whom I shall name."

Naturally Lizzie hesitated, since the complete freedom
to act as she willed was of paramount importance to her.
But to have her work so supported and her name known
by the intervention of the great critic!

She bent her burnished head.

And then she said, "It shall be as you say."

Later, distrusting Lizzie's strength as much as he distrusted her ability, Gabriel opted for the annual subsidy.

"I cannot like her," the lady of the house said. "Henry, I try to like her but I do not."

"It isn't worthy of you," Dr. Acland said austerely. "You know how much she is in need of kindness." And then because he was not by nature an austere man, he put his arm about the wife of his bosom and hugged her warmly. "Try again," he suggested. "When the opportunity presents itself."

Mollified, she sniffed. "Oh, the opportunity will present itself," she said. "Daily."

"Not today at least, my love," he said with some satisfaction. "Today the warden of New College is showing her the manuscripts in the Bodleian. It's his turn."

The Sid at Oxford? Yes.

Here, in that peerless city caressed by both the Thames and the Cherwell as they meandered the water meadows and breathed forth pearly diaphanous mists from which the spires arose and through which the bells reverberated — Oxford, the grey home of wisdom — here she was, walking in her strange clothes and with her strange thoughts up and down High Street and Queen, Cornmarket and Saint Aldgates, and learning that one spoke of these streets as "the Corn" and "Saint Olds" and of the little river as "the Char." Silent as ever and as remote and turning the heads of the scholars with her cold gold beauty.

Lizzie Siddal, the bonnet maker from the Kent Road, an honoured guest at Oxford? Yes indeed, and not behaving very well, either. That very day she did not appear at the Bodleian, because the warden of New College bored and offended her. Upon the last occasion he had shown her a black beetle as painted by Albrecht Dürer and then for purposes of comparison, sent down to the kitchens for a real one.

No doubt the warden of New College should have known better, yet there were surely better ways for Lizzie to display her displeasure. Gabriel would not have liked it. Gabriel had called the warden "that great swell," had proudly reported to their friends that she was "greatly bothered with attentions" and that she moved "in all the best society."

As so she did. The ladies, on the whole, were charmed by her demeanour, which in company could be gentle as a dove, and the gentlemen by her quick mind and reputed talents. Her hostess noticed that she seemed most drawn to Dr. Pusey, though whether it was because the eminent divine had replaced John Henry Newman, after that gentleman's apostasy to Rome, as the renowned leader of the Oxford Movement or because he was an inconsolable widower, one cannot be sure. Lizzie was ever drawn to thoughts of separation and the grave.

Gabriel himself had supplied Dr. Acland with the evidence of her deteriorating health. Dr. Garth Wilkinson, the famous Swedenborgian and editor of Blake, had said that Lizzie suffered from "curvature of the spine" and had called it "a most anxious case." And then for good measure, Gabriel reported that a prominent London physician (whom he did not further identify) had warned that one lung was severely affected.

Now it happened that Dr. Henry Acland, Reader in Anatomy at Oxford, Fellow of Christ Church and of All Souls, and friend to John Ruskin, was a man whose rampant generosity prevented him from distinguishing between his professional and personal life. Of course he would attend Ruskin's unfortunate young friend who, furthermore, should make free of his house by day or night. This may have been why Mrs. Acland could not like her; on the whole, ladies do not care even for gentlemen who make free of their houses by day or night.

Indeed, she was only partially assuaged when in return

to some mild complaint, John Ruskin wrote to her, "I don't know exactly how that wilful Ida has behaved to you. As far as I can make out, she is not ungrateful but sick, and sickly headstrong."

Ida, indeed! For in naming her for Mr. Tennyson's heroine Ruskin implied that Lizzie was a savant and a princess; perhaps no woman likes to hear another woman so acclaimed.

But Mrs. Acland was compassionate and a fit mate for her warmhearted and impractical spouse. Accustomed to binding up the injured susceptibilities of undergraduates, eager to ease the old, the sick, the frail, ready as a nurse to support her husband with a hot poultice, a basin, or a smile — if Lizzie had once turned to her, had once coughed for her, had once acknowledged their mutual womanhood!

But Lizzie was very grand and very aloof. And she was also very frightened and very young. Because of her thin height, her gaunt beauty, and the length of time her name had been associated with Gabriel's, most thought her older than she was. William Michael Rossetti never took to her but was a just and not unkindly youth; he thought that when she was at Oxford she was no more than twenty-one, though about that he was mistaken. But inexperienced she was, and defensive. She could not be sure that the warden of New College was not reminding her that on the Kent Road, black beetles abounded.

And Gabriel, upon whom she had come to depend so much, was not with her. She was again deposited alone in lodgings with her old striped silk and with the knowledge, or at least the belief, that all this interest in her sprang from just two things: Gabriel's drawings of her, which proved him an artist, and her own drawings — which proved her a curiosity.

The evening came when she got out the laudanum drops again. She sat with her thin, bare feet against the little fender and the ashy fire where the cannel coal burned dimly, and with bitter honesty she faced the fact that Gabriel loved her. But not as she needed to be loved. He wanted only that she remain the will-o'-the-wisp, the unattainable, *La Belle Dame Sans Merci. Beata Beatrix*, and thus betrayed.

Slowly she leafed through the drawings that in her heart she knew Ruskin was going to buy, not to reward her, but to relieve Gabriel. They had been nice to her at Oxford. Dr. Pusey's maiden sisters had been cordial as that good man himself; Mrs. Acland's hospitality disguised itself as warm; many were curious and many, like the shy undergraduates who were dumb before her, honestly admired. But only Dr. Acland not only cared for her but cared to care, took her for long walks into the countryside and talked to her, not as a patient, but as a friend.

Like a good child, she began to draw a picture for him.

The day came when Dr. Acland told her.

She couldn't stay on in Oxford indefinitely, and there was very little he could do for her.

It was a pewter-coloured day; the mists rolled sluggishly along the rivers and the sun hung thin and dull. It was a fit day for the saying of last things. Lizzie shivered in a grey linsey-woolsey. She had not been before in Dr. Acland's study; since it was not the time of year for fires, there was no fire. And he did not seem the same person that he seemed in the drawing room or on those comfortable walks when he had not pressed her failing breath too hard and had, instead of scolding and exhorting, pointed out with glee the chalk-coloured sheep by their charcoal-coloured pens.

He had not harried or frightened her in any way, as her new friend had promised that he would not do. For she had balked and sulked until John Ruskin had promised, "Only put your tongue out once and let him feel your pulse."

But that was not all he had done. He had spoken to her; not as if she were an invalid or an artist's encumbrance or a difficult guest. He had spoken to Elizabeth Siddal.

Today he seemed distant and oracular.

That was a busy room; one could hardly see an inch of tabletop nor of embossed wallpaper for the evidence of grateful patients: crewelwork, framed testimonials, daguerreotypes, crocheting and embroideries and countless gift volumes; doubtless, since almost everyone he knew was a scholar in some field, each bore a famous name. Her long glance slid from one object to another while she waited for him to speak.

He had, she thought as she had thought before, nice, broad, hairy hands with plump paternal fingers into whose grasp you would entrust a lancet or a greenstick fracture. At the moment those broad hands moved slowly — though not as slowly as it seemed to her — over his mounded notes and papers. While she waited she did what everyone does while waiting. Much as she treasured the idea of death, she thought: *it cannot be*.

And then she thought, why not? And in that dread eventuality, would she have done anything differently in the past? But how could she have done except as she had done?

She said, "Then I am going to die?"

Dr. Acland was shocked, not so much by the familiar question as by its conversational tone, as if she asked, "Then it will rain, you think?"

"My dear young woman," he said crossly. "Eventually, one supposes. But no matter what you may have been told, I find no evidence that your lungs are affected. Your posture, only, creates a curvature; your heart is strong and regular. Your nerves are bad."

She found to her surprise that what she felt was consternation, though she was far from convinced that he was right.

"True, you are not robust," he said more gently. "But Miss Siddal — Lizzie — there is no reason why you should not marry. And raise a healthy family too, what's more."

She smiled at him, but remotely. He had no way of knowing that he was robbing her of her strongest hold upon Gabriel's loyalty. Naturally she did not wish to die: she only wished that others might think that she might. Now she would have to find another weapon. Since she would not hold Gabriel with her body, she would have to hold him through his pride.

"Mind you," said Dr. Acland, "you should live very quietly. Avoid excitement, worry, and concern."

How?

"Maintain good habits and refrain from all but simple diets. Fresh air, gentle exercise . . ."

But she must draw harder, paint harder, write harder; force the world to acknowledge her as an artist in her own right. She must.

"This is for you," she said.

She had drawn the chalk-coloured sheep and the sheep-fold. Beyond, she had added a tombstone and a spire. Perhaps the country churchyard led her to hope that Dr. Acland's gentle soul would hold her in loving thought when she was gone.

No two people ever saw Elizabeth Siddal alike.

Dr. Acland wrote to his friend John Ruskin that he had found her "a kindly, gentle, quiet person." And he believed, he said, the true cause of her illness to be "mental power long pent up and lately over-taxed."

He had no doubt, he said, that from now on she would follow only the most quiet and restful of pursuits.

12

IT WAS A GREAT source of pride to Fanny Cornforth that she had a key to Chatham Place — although she was to use it with discretion. This was because Lizzie also had a key and, since she had become engaged, used it often; in fact she sometimes stayed there during Gabriel's absences, which startled Fanny.

What she herself did was all right because she was a married woman.

Fanny Cornforth had been little more than a child when she married and had never had any reason to regret it, although her husband was a sot. As drunkards go, however, he was a pleasant one, given to loud song and sudden sleep and not inclined to play the tyrant to his young wife. And in this he was wise, for Fanny liked her own way but, in her own way, was faithful; she never grudged him the odd shilling, she nursed him through his horrors and did not refuse him the medicinal drop.

Fanny was careful to hide from Gabriel that she loved

him. She was a big, ripe girl, and clever: if he cared to think her favours easily come by, let him — at least he would not be frightened.

And as a matter of fact, he found her restful. She had no fear of retribution, while he, whose childhood had been saturated in Dante Alighieri, was haunted still by the steep circles of Hell. He had asked her once why she was not afraid, but she misunderstood: he spoke of a vengeful God and she thought he meant her husband.

"You mean get back at me?" she asked. "Why should he?" And she laughed her rich, bubbling laughter. "I give him a good day's work. Yes, and a good night's, too!"

But then, Fanny was not much interested in herself. Not that she did not know what she wanted and was not ingenious in procuring it; Fanny was light-fingered. But though shrewd, she was brave and loyal to her curious commitments, and she had nothing of Lizzie's exhausting self-concern. Had Gabriel confided to her any of Lizzie's painful anxieties and niceties, he dared say he knew what she would answer.

"Cor!" she would say. "What a ninny!"

Meantime, as he tired of his early religiosities, he found her increasingly pleasant to paint. Those creamy colors! The fair, heavy hair tumbling about the luscious breast and shoulders! The rich silks and velvets clung to her limbs like caresses; above, the soft, full mouth and sly, blue eyes mocked, laughed, and invited.

Gabriel was always to be clever about entitling these paintings, knowing instinctively that a puzzled British public might accept a *Bocca Baciatta* but would wheel in fright from *The Kissed Mouth*. About other things he was not clever but a jumble of contradictions: both cautious and rebellious, foresighted and prodigal, docile and hard to curb as a spirited horse.

This it was that John Ruskin meant when he said

sharply, "You inventive people pay dearly for your power — there is no knowing how to manage you."

And yet Fanny Cornforth thought that, better than most, she could manage Gabriel.

On a dark, dreary evening of a year that followed by some time John Ruskin's espousal of Lizzie's fortune, Gabriel glared into his mirror at Chatham Place. He was a disappointed man. Everyone knew his name. But why didn't he make any tin?

Here he was at twenty-seven, which is going on twenty-eight, which is almost thirty. His dark, lovesome locks were getting a little high. He had never been as tall as Holman Hunt nor as fresh-coloured as Brown nor as winsome as Johnny Millais, and if he were not careful he would soon have a little belly.

Fanny Cornforth put her round, white arms about him and said, "Ah, come off it, Rizzetty!"

On the other hand his eyes were brilliant as ever and everybody knew his name.

He gave her soft waist an affectionate hug.

At least everyone who counted. The tinker would have said, "*Who?*" And so would the baker and the tailor, although the greengrocer down the way had reason to remember. Harley Street did not yet know his name, nor was it bruited about Threadneedle. But among those conversant with such things he was called the leader of the Pre-Raphaelites, although almost no one yet owned his work, because he did not produce very much of it and refused to exhibit lest he be attacked.

If he had ever come close to losing his coterie (he did come close to losing his coterie) it was when he refused to show in their rebellious exhibition. Some of them had not been accepted by the Academy judges, and those who were accepted had found their paintings "skied"; no spec-

tator was avid enough to crane his neck against the bad
light and the inconvenient height. Indignant and confident, the PRB had held their own show, but their leader
was not represented.

Unfortunately, John Millais was. Upon *Christ in the
House of Joseph the Carpenter* the critics whetted their
knives. His mother cried.

"Johnny," she said, "I understand he is not even English!"

Gabriel had not meant to let them down, but he had
honestly believed that were his name associated with theirs,
they would become vulnerable to his foes. Just as his
father flattered himself that he was ringed by political
enemies, Gabriel believed himself besieged by the envious.

Tonight he was trying to dress for dinner at the Browns
and was in a hurry, this being something of an occasion:
it was the first time in a week that Lizzie had deigned to
meet him.

While Emma Brown was not a demanding hostess, he
felt it would be impolitic to be late, and Chatham Place
was a chaos of yesterday's teacups, smoky lamps, flung
clothing, and cigar ash. Gabriel snatched up a white thing
in hope that it would prove to be his stock; it was an infant's napkin, acrid and dry. For the Browns had been
around the previous evening in the role of peacemakers.

"Damn it," he said, "this place is become a sty!" And he
looked speculatively at Fanny Cornforth.

"Not a chance, old dear. I'm not your scrub-lady." She
laughed, good-natured. "Better get some old biddy in, if
you can find one who'll work on spec. Or better yet, make
up the quarrel and let her ladyship wash up."

He said, "You're impertinent. And you eat too much."

Yes, she did. Those delicious rotundities were coarsen-
ing and the round chin threatened to be heavy; already,
when he painted her, he was forced to diminish her.

"Ah well," Fanny said comfortably, "you know I love to eat. And anyway, Hughes likes a proper armful."

Gabriel grinned. "He has good taste," he said.

But watching him wrap himself against the night she suddenly said, "Rizzetty."

"Yes?" he said. "Yes?"

But nothing in the streets had taught her how to say "I love you" — even had that been wise.

So instead she said, gazing at him with those round, sapphire eyes, "Whyn'cha give her a clout?"

Imagine clouting a woman who has established, somehow, a moral ascendancy over you?

But as he clattered down the stairs and out into the inclement night, he did resent the tyranny that drove him out of his warm rooms. For the night was frightful; the wind, in a temper, lashed like a termagant's tongue, and the signs over the shop doors shook and swung. A cold rain hurled itself in sheets, blowing along the gutters, drumming along the roofs; it wound the skirts of Gabriel's coat around his knees and found each crevice, however tiny, between boot and trouser, hat brim and coat collar. He shivered, facing into it now and feeling it strike his face like a blow.

Damn Lizzie. Ever since she had returned from France she had been impossible.

Perhaps he should have thought more of the monotony of her days over the apothecary, after Oxford and the companionship of gentlefolk. Was she who had been so much admired now to sit alone and wait his pleasure, to dandle another woman's baby and bend in solitude over the fey and melancholy drawings with which she earned her living?

Oh she was, was she!

Furthermore, when Gabriel pointed out that Lizzie was

behaving childishly, even ungratefully, for a young woman who had just, so to speak, been presented with a new lease on life, Emma looked troubled.

"Something is wrong," she said. "It may not be her lungs, but Gabriel, she is not well."

Then he would become irate, and in fact rather blamed the Browns for encouraging Lizzie's perversities. Ruskin, however, thought that perhaps a change of scene? . . . And Ruskin was, moreover, willing to augment her stipend for the purpose, although in return he did expect to have his opinions honoured; he wanted her to go to Italy or to Switzerland, where the soft somnolent airs of the one might lull her fevered temperament or the grandeur of the other impress upon her the fatuousness of human desire.

Now Lizzie wished to go to Paris.

But Ruskin felt that the nervous tempo and the brilliant life of Paris could only exacerbate all that was sickly in Lizzie, so other arrangements were made. Naturally Gabriel was to remain in England. It was unthinkable that a single lady should be accompanied by her fiancé; besides, he had other plans for Gabriel, who he hoped while unencumbered would put in a period of serious and uninterrupted work. He was tiring of Gabriel's dilatory ways and embarrassed by the complaints of those whom he had badgered into giving the young man commissions. A Mrs. Kincaid would go with her. This Mrs. Kincaid did not promise to be a scintillating companion but enjoyed the advantage of being a sort of female connection of the Rossettis and so might be looked upon as a first wedge into Lizzie's acceptance by the family. So lodgings were taken for them at Nice and Lizzie, once her remittance was in hand, went straight to Paris, where she was happier than she had been for some time.

She had no entrée anywhere and lived in a modest pension where the table was simple, but to Lizzie the shops, the avenues, the sight of fashionable and wealthy people were a delight, as was the fact that she herself was watched and was delightful. Many a well-dressed gentleman turned to observe the flame-haired *Anglaise* in her new clothes. For Lizzie put aside the old striped silk and donned the new hoopskirts introduced by the empress Eugénie de Montijo, and since new skirts demand new bonnets and laces and reticules and parasols, she soon had to send home for more money and, in fact, was much in debt.

Ruskin said only: "It has been my experience that people do not admit all their debts. See if you can find out in just how much disorder her affairs are."

Relieved by a bank draught, Lizzie again wrote gay, even frivolous letters; then her letters ceased. Gabriel was at first alarmed lest she be ill and then lest her pursuit of pleasure cause her to be ill. He laboured for a week, eschewing all distractions, completed a fine water-colour and what's more sold it, and with the proceeds followed her to France.

It was then — and for the first time in their married life — that Hughes saw Fanny Cornforth cry. She was not living with him at the time, for Gabriel Rossetti had set her up in Wapping, in quarters of her own, and her Hughes found her sprawling on her unmade bed and pummeling the pillows with her fists.

"He'll marry her," she said. "You'll see — she'll get him yet!"

He was relieved to see that they were tears of rage.

"Never mind, love; he'll never do without you. So what's the odds?" he said.

And indeed in France, for a time, Gabriel and Lizzie were happy; he found her at once more animated, affectionate, incandescent, so much so that a sculptor friend

who encountered them by accident hurried to report at
home that "Rossetti seems much in love as ever."

And Gabriel was having a ripping time. He called on
the Brownings, who were in residence in Paris at the time,
and was received graciously, if with some surprise. Lizzie
did not fret that she did not join them. She preferred not
to meet anyone from home and was content to be seen by
strangers, who might think that she sprang from Mayfair
and not from the Kent Road.

Alas, all games must end, and the day came when the
trunks must be packed and they must follow Mrs. Kincaid (with whom Lizzie had early quarreled) back to
England. One supposes that Mrs. Kincaid had lost no
time in communicating to her connections that the im-
petuous son and brother, without regard to appearances
or to the comfort of Mrs. Kincaid, had followed his friend
to Paris.

Now the bad times began again.

For one thing, Ruskin, on whom so much of their present comfort and future hope depended, grew cool. "Nin-
nies," he called them.

"I am ill-tempered today," he wrote to Gabriel. "You
are such absurd creatures both of you. I don't say you do
wrong, because you don't seem to know what *is* wrong,
but just to do whatever you like as far as possible — as
puppies and tomtits do."

Lizzie Siddal did not like that letter and she did not
forget it.

Deprived of her new pleasures she grew pensive first
and then sullen, and Gabriel, oppressed by her demands,
escaped more and more often to a place where Lizzie could
not follow, and of which she could not legitimately complain.

The Working Men's College in Red Lion Square was
a particular interest of John Ruskin's; he felt that both

his wealth and wit required such interest of him. He was much encouraged to find that the workingmen of England were curious about art, and not averse to turning out a bit of it themselves, and since Gabriel's knowledge in this field was more practical than his own — although not by much — Ruskin prevailed upon him to participate.

At first Gabriel was taken aback by this request and turned to Brown for help. "Will you oblige me with a few words," he wrote, "as to the way you consider best for getting the colourmen to lay a white ground on canvas?" And then admitted, "I know you have told me 100 times, but I never can remember that sort of thing."

Armed with this aid, Gabriel saw a way to both please his patron and protect a few evenings for himself: for if he claimed to be at the college, who was to say he wasn't? And while his attendance might be erratic, the working-men liked and respected him. He didn't cramp them at classic casts, but had each turn and draw the man beside him.

"The British mug," he said, "is the finer of the two."

And he put on no airs. No, they would not have peached on him, even if they had known to whom to peach.

But Lizzie had a way of throwing back her head and looking with cold amusement when he mentioned the college that made him uneasy even when he had actually been there, and worse, she had also begun to rant and rail, which she had never done before, and had been known to throw herself upon the Browns' hearth rug and shriek.

"I really think that you make a mistake," Emma Brown would tell him. "If you press her, there is no telling what Lizzie may do."

Tonight she was waiting for him — cold, distant, and determined, an ice-maiden, white of face but with green eyes gleaming with . . . what? Triumph. Triumphant women always made him uncomfortable. What did they have to be triumphant about? His mother and his sisters sometimes looked that way.

Meantime, around an enthroned Lizzie, domestic chaos prevailed. Emma Brown was a pretty woman, and a dear woman, though rather a silly woman, but she was a bad housekeeper. The house was small, the paraphernalia of her husband's profession overflowed, the lamps smoked, and Gabriel could find no place to put his sopped coat. Brown took it from him, looked about hopelessly, and then supported it upon the fender, from which it spread in a tide of wet wool. In one corner where the shadows clustered, the new baby snuffled and wailed as if appalled to consider its own prospects.

Gabriel approached his bride-to-be and bent above her hand. She was in one of her crisp moods that emphasized her efficiency.

"Don't be silly, Gug," she said, but not unkindly.

Brown and his Emma slid hopeful glances at one another. And if all did not go merrily as a wedding bell, conversationally speaking the two antagonists circled warily about one another; it was not until an intimidated young person in a mobcap had brought up supper (which was chops) that it became apparent that one of the circlers had only been waiting an opportunity to attack. Then Gabriel provided that opening, having been lulled by the gentle tenor of the conversation, and in an instant she was at him.

"I suppose you've been all right for tin?" he asked. "Heard this month from Ruskin, have you? Yes?"

Elizabeth Siddal dropped her lashes over the sparkling emerald eyes.

"Yes," she said. "For the last time."

"What do you mean, for the last time? What have you done to offend him, Lizzie?"

He was horrified. For a long time, the one thing that had made their uneasy alliance possible was her financial independence. Freighted with anger and low at the bow with want, their small bark needed only the one cold comber of her need to founder and capsize.

"He shall hear from me," Gabriel said hotly. "I took him for a man of his word."

"Oh, *Ruskin* keeps his word," she said dangerously.

In the corner the infant coughed and cried and Emma rose gratefully and flew to the cradle.

Now Gabriel's voice was dangerous. "What have you done, Lizzie?"

"Only what any honest woman would."

"And what am I to make of that?"

"We had a contract. I cannot fulfill it."

"And why?"

She raised her eyes and shot him an accusing look.

"Aha! You mean your health forbids," he said.

"It does indeed."

Then if she could not care for herself he must care for her.

"Emma," he said, "are you behind this?"

But he knew she wasn't. Emma was too well acquainted with want and worry to have offered such advice. In her defense her husband prepared to speak and then, being a man of sense as well as kindliness, he didn't. Instead, he offered to pass the peas. Now Gabriel seemed to see in this inflammatory suggestion a personal affront, and glaring first at his old friend, he then leaned to his lady.

Stung by nervous exasperation and real concern he said, "You imply that I destroy your health. But it is not your health that prevents your little efforts, Lizzie, but the lamentable fact that you have no talent."

The cold rain spoke against the windows. The wind grieved at the door for admittance and then, angered to be refused, buffeted the thin, old walls and shook the shutters.

Elizabeth Siddal rose and left the room. The others

looked at one another in consternation; then in another moment the door slammed and she was gone into the night.

Emma clapped her small, worn hands to her mouth. "Oh, Gabriel," she cried. "After her!"

He said, "I will not."

"But she is frail and has been coughing much of late; she will be chill and drenched. Gabriel, she will do herself a harm! If you cannot catch her, follow to be sure that she is warm and dry — she will sit wet by a cold hearth — I know her!"

"I know her too," he said. "I will not follow."

Emma looked at her husband's friend with hatred.

"Then if you won't go," she said, "I will."

She sprang like a cat and before the men had clumsily pushed back their chairs and risen she was bonneted; she snatched the baby from the cradle and swathing it in her shawl, turned to the door. Then Brown was at her side and grasped her wrist. Against her shoulder the baby bobbed.

He said, "You can't do this."

Goodness knows that poor Brown had done nothing to precipitate her fury, but at such times all men become the enemy.

Emma said, "Let me go!"

He did. The wind soughed briefly through the open door and set the lamp flames shuddering. Then the door banged. Brown turned back, rubbing his hair and muttering.

Gabriel said icily, "Cannot you control your wife?"

Brown dropped himself into his chair and his head into his hands.

"Wherever you go, Gabriel," he said, "wrath and disorder go with you." Then he said, "My dear old friend. I should not have said that."

But Gabriel was deeply wounded by the words and deeply troubled lest they be true.

Brown kicked moodily at the table leg. "Emma means

well," he said. "I cannot claim she used her head. You see, the child has the croup."

Gabriel looked at him in horror. "And took it out on such a night? And still you did not stop her?"

"And what was I to do? Wrestle with her like Jacob with the angel?"

"You could at least have kept the child."

"How? And she nursing?"

Both men subsided into unhappy silence. How could it be that loving Brown so well, Gabriel could have brought upon him such distress? Soothing though it would be to name it Lizzie's fault, he could not claim it was entirely Lizzie's fault. No, it was a rum go. And Gabriel, who all his life had had only the merest nodding acquaintance with philosophy, pondered these things.

For Lizzie — who when she first came to him had given so generously of such bright gifts: her clear laughter and quick wit and her wild beauty — had now, like the wicked fairy at the christening, brought him the gift of guilt.

And indeed, later she cried to him, "Murderer!"
Because the Browns' little baby did not live.

13

ONE EVENING AT THE Working Men's College,
Gabriel, charcoal in hand, looked up from a drawing he was savagely correcting. A strange young man was
gazing at him.

He gazed fiercely back.

Whoever the fellow was, he was no workingman, for
in spite of his burly shoulders and unkempt cap of curls,
he had the mien and boots of a gentleman and no right to
be present in this place, disrupting the hours and efforts
of the poor and the dedicated. Another glance showed
Gabriel a face of singular guilelessness; why, the chap
was not much more than a stripling, and the fact first
filled Gabriel with rage and then with melancholy.

Five years before, he himself had been the stripling,
filled with faith and the promise of his own promise. What
was he now? A harassed man with a bit of a name, pub-
licly exposed to the curiosity of this youngster like a wom-
bat at the zoo. Or worse, perhaps the stranger was not
curious at all but had been sent by some tradesman to
dun him for an unpaid bill.

"Take care," Christina had told him recently. "Our

father suffered from the illusion that unfriendly eyes were on him. But Gabriel, he *had* made enemies." She ran her long, inky hand affectionately across his brow. "Your enemies are here."

Perhaps. But inimical or not, this stranger trespassed. Gabriel snapped and threw down the charcoal and, striding to the back of the room, challenged him.

"What the devil do you want?"

The stranger flushed to the roots of his wild, dark hair. He said, "My name is William Morris. I'm an architect — well, of sorts. I thought . . . I hoped . . ."

And in fact what he had hoped was to behold the tower of flesh wherein genius dwelt. Because he and his friend considered Gabriel Rossetti the genius of the age, and since they were about to publish a small magazine, not unlike *The Germ*, they dared to hope that the poet would honour their pages with one of his miraculous poems . . .

Gabriel said, "How old are you?"

"Twenty-two."

Gabriel felt his veins knot with rage. Six years, *only six years*, younger than himself, and mocking him with the show of respect due a sage and pundit! Then he remembered old Brown and the walking stick and his own boyish sincerity. This William Morris gazed at him with the fervid and slightly glazed eyes of the true disciple.

In spite of himself, Gabriel was mollified. Warm winds of self-esteem blew about him. There is all the difference in the world between impertinence and homage.

"I shall be here another hour," he said. "Then if you like, I can offer you a cup of tea or a glass of something."

Thus casually did these two meet who would be intimates, and each of whom would rob the other of the dearest treasure of his life.

"What's he like?" asked Ned Jones.

Edward Jones, who later began to call himself Burne-

Jones (and little wonder), was a frail fellow with soft, lank hair and a fine eye.

"Oh, a prince!" William Morris said.

Ned Jones and Topsy Morris had met at Oxford and had become Damon and Pythias, alike in circumstance as they were unlike in body; both were idealists, both romantics, both had gone through a period of religious enthusiasm, and both were the happy possessors of comfortable incomes, thanks to the perspicacity of their parents.

"He's giving us a ripping ballad." And Topsy began to intone:

> Heavenborn Helen, Sparta's queen,
> (*O Troy Town!*)
> Had two breasts of heavenly sheen,
> The sun and moon of the heart's desire;
> All Love's lordship lay between.
> (*O Troy's down,*
> *Tall Troy's on fire!*)

"You don't think," Ned said nervously, "that it's a little . . ."

Morris looked at him with affectionate contempt.

"To publish Rossetti in the *Oxford and Cambridge Magazine*," he said, "I would risk anything." And he read on to the end.

> Paris turned upon his bed
> (*O Troy Town!*)
> Turned upon his bed and said,
> Dead at heart with the heart's desire —
> "O to clasp her golden head!"
> (*O Troy's down,*
> *Tall Troy's on fire!*)

By that time Ned Jones also was ignited.

William Morris had been marked for great things from

childhood and had been much indulged, perhaps because he had been frail and the only son in a covey of daughters. He read at an age to disquiet parents and by four was familiar with all the Waverley novels; at six his father, a partner in a London brokerage, bought him a pony and had made for him a little suit of armour, in which he rode the aisles of Epping Forest dreaming of lords and ladies. And when he was thirteen his father died and left him monarch of the house.

By all that was reasonable the spoiled darling should have turned out a wastrel, but nothing about Morris was ever reasonable. He proved a devoted son and a cautious brother and only once disappointed his mother (though that grievously), when on the advice of Gabriel Rossetti he gave up the office of the architect to dabble in the arts.

But first at Oxford he had, with Ned Jones, considered first the clergy and then a lay brotherhood where, with congenial friends, they could pursue theology and medieval poetry. For poetry was a persisting enthusiasm of them both and on many an evening they would, in the company of other excitable youths, sport the oak and read by the hour to one another.

One night Topsy Morris said, "I think I can do that, too."

The very next night he said modestly, "I call it *The Defence of Guenevere*," and began.

> But, knowing now that they would have her speak,
> She threw her wet hair backward from her brow,
> Her hand close to her mouth touching her cheek,
> As though she had had there a shameful blow . . .

Line after loose, melodious line, one hundred and twenty-four of them in all, galloped along until he finished:

"All I have said is truth, by Christ's dear tears."

They were dumb with admiration.

"It isn't hard," said William Morris modestly.

Now dangers attend the inability to abandon Alma Mater, that first seductress of gentle youth. Had Ned and Topsy not been drawn back to Oxford they might not have become aware of the irresistible opportunity presented by the Union Debating Society's new building. There in the great hall were four tall, bare walls and ten deep bays, still wet with gleaming plaster, that cried out for decoration. What could be better than Sir Thomas Malory and *Le Morte d'Arthur*? And who should be better to execute it than themselves, under the aegis and direction of Dante Gabriel Rossetti, who would tell them how?

Important dons, innocent of such matters, caught fire; Gabriel himself was delighted. He had always wanted to do murals, about which he knew very little, and he felt that tempera might be easier than oils. He was flattered to be recognized as the doyen of these talented young men, and then he always liked to get away from London. They volunteered their services and the dons guaranteed their expenses, and it was summertime; the long days were filled with company and work, the evenings were bright with song and laughter.

What a lark!

Ned Jones was at first a little worried; though they were lovers of art, poetry, and the past, they were not professionals.

Topsy was confident. "Gabriel says I shall be able to paint," he said.

There was some difficulty about models. As Arthur, Modred, Lancelot, they could pose for one another, but women were a problem. For Guinevere and Iseult, Gabriel said firmly that Lizzie would not do. A Juno was needed, not a dryad.

And Juno appeared.

Will Little found her, but this time not by accident.

It was some time since Will had had any opportunity to intervene in his friend's life. He had made an uneasy truce with Lizzie: he had had to. But he resented these young men in whose company Gabriel became so young.

The very first day Will was in Oxford, Gabriel, who was balanced upon a high stepladder with his paintpots, called down to him, "Watch out!"

There was of course no time to watch out, and Will got the better part of a jar of lapis lazuli on his new coat; the new coat was expensive and so was the lapis lazuli.

"Never mind," said Gabriel airily. "There's plenty more where that came from."

Topsy Morris laughed and Will whirled and looked at him severely. Morris was also teetering on a ladder and drawing the cartoon for the bay assigned as his responsibility. The foreground of the cartoon seemed to consist of nothing but gigantic sunflowers behind which gigantic figures loomed.

"I can't get the feet right," Morris explained cheerfully.

His heart throbbing with indignation, Will Little went back to his inn, divested himself of his ruined clothing, and freshly dressed went out to prove himself indispensable.

The Oxford streets in the long holidays were empty, but he supposed there must be females about; the trick was to find them. Ordinarily he would have begun by looking for whores; there are strong and interesting types among them. But there didn't seem to be any whores about; perhaps with the young gentlemen out of town there was little call for them or perhaps — he was not really familiar with Oxford — they were not allowed. At any rate, the only women he saw upon the streets were elderly matrons with shopping bags and, to be sure, a peppering of bluestockings.

He did not think the daughters of dons would prove suitable.

So he went in and out of shops, pretending a need for pins and ribbons, for bloaters and rutabagas and for *The Times*, all of which he did indeed carry off. There were young women behind many counters and some of them were pretty, or very nearly pretty, but none were interesting: one had a delicate colour, one a clean, bright smile, and several of them had hair, but there were no good bones beneath.

Accordingly, he strolled to the edge of town, where in the lanes or fields some farmer's healthy girl might be espied. The day was fine, the air clear and cool, and a meadowlark sprang spiraling from a field of grain. He heard a countryman's voice lifted in imprecation and the calm comment of cows; the lark sang, pure and detached. Then ahead and hidden by hedgerows he heard horses and in a moment saw three horsewomen riding abreast. He stepped quickly aside and they dropped courteously into single file.

One was Juno the Ox-Eyed.

They were obviously sisters and they were all good-looking girls, but the first sat her saddle like a tall queen, her broad shoulders straight, one boot showing a gleaming toe beneath the voluminous folds of her habit, one gloved hand holding her crop like a wand. From under her glossy hat sprang her amazing hair: coarse-fibred, vigorously curling in a cloud of jetty black. Her air was haughty and even cold, but as he hastened to tip his hat she did incline her head, though gravely. Her sisters, either younger or lighter of heart, smiled pleasantly, the beat of hooves quickened, and they swept by.

Will Little's heart drummed in his waistcoat. He had done it again.

It was not hard in a town the size of Oxford to find out who she was. She was a Miss Jane Burden; her father was the owner of a livery stable and was held in high regard by his fellow citizens. He himself had a high regard both for the university and for anyone who was profitably connected with it. Yes, his daughter — if she so chose — might sit for Mr. Rossetti and his friends. The place was public, the painters gentry, the paintings decorous.

Jane Burden did so choose. She found the admiration of the young gentlemen acceptable, the more so perhaps because not everyone admired her. Some found her full, protuberant red lips provocative; to others they seemed coarse. Her brows met in an angry bar above her nose. Either she had great dignity or else she was sullen or silent for want of anything to say. Some thought her of a stately height; to some she was a great gawk of a girl. Gabriel thought her strange hair luxuriant; to others it seemed unkempt. As for her temperament — was she kind, was she able, would she prove patient and true? No one could tell. Jane Burden didn't say.

One thing the world had to agree. As Gabriel Rossetti painted her, she had a dark and ominous beauty.

Topsy Morris was all unfit to fall in love. Nothing in his life had prepared him for that most dangerous of emotions. An alarming part of the legacy his father had left him was the true conviction that the world is honest, friends faithful, women virtuous. His mother was virtuous and his sisters nice-looking, wholesome, even-tempered girls, but nothing about them readied him to meet in person her whom he had known all his life in dreams.

By now the great hall that had gleamed white as a snow castle glowed and throbbed with colour; along the

walls and in and out of the ten big bays the knights and
ladies stalked, the cuirasses and greaves shone gold and
silver, the robes of the maidens flowed bright as living
lava. Jane Burden, dressed in peacock blue and scarlet,
paced among the artists and rested from her pose.

His liege lady, the keeper of his soul, the only woman
to whom he would want to bring his fortune and his heart.
But how to tell her? She was uncommunicative and he was
shy. Before, he had been too busy. Besides, he didn't feel
that he could say anything so intimate to her, not with the
others coming and going with their pots and brushes,
swaying upon their ladders and crying down their jests. So,
scooping up from the clutter at his feet a slate upon which
he had scrawled

> gamboge
> vermilion and
> old rags

he wiped it hastily with the elbow of his jacket and grasped
a bit of chalk.

"I love you," Topsy wrote.

Flushing furiously, he put it into her long, cool hands.
She read it and smiled slightly. Then she stepped back
upon the dais and reassumed her pose.

William Morris climbed back to his labours, satisfied.
He had been brave; he had been honest. Far below him
Gabriel swore softly, jumped to the dais, and began to
rearrange the folds of Jane's bright, heavy robes. She
straightened her square shoulders and lifted her head with
its explosion of dark hair and Gabriel put his hand upon
her cheek and turned her face to his.

"There," he said. "Like that."

From above, Topsy did not see the way their eyes met,
like a blow.

14

A**T JUST ABOUT** that same time, Lizzie herself acquired a young admirer. This was Algernon Charles Swinburne, an astonishing youth and the scion of a family of noble birth and great wealth, though he did not think much of the one and could get his hands on precious little of the other.

A great believer in freedom and equality, he loved Elizabeth Siddal because she behaved as though she were free and equal and because she was, as he described her, "a most lovable creature, brilliant and appreciative," with eyes "coloured like the water-flower and deeper than the green sea's glass." By which it may be seen that the young man was by way of being a poet. And then, they both were white of skin and carrot-haired and they both needed someone very much.

But he was not in love with The Sid. Indeed, he was never in love but with one person, and she was his first cousin. Her family, because of the consanguinity and also because Swinburne was small and odd and had attacks of a nervous disorder, married her to an older and more stable man.

His parents were both of aristocratic stock. Admiral Swinburne's ancestor had received a baronetcy in 1660, "*virum, patrimonio censu et morum probitate spectabilem.*" Of Sir John, Swinburne's grandfather, it had been said that "the two maddest things in the north country were his horse and himself," and Swinburne, who adored him, said proudly of him that "he was a friend of the great Turner," and added, "I wish to God he had discovered Blake."

His mother was Lady Jane Henrietta, daughter of George, the third earl of Ashburnham. She, like his father, worried about their eccentric and excitable son. When he had those attacks his arms jerked and his hands fluttered, while his small, white face wore a look of radiant rapture. The physician whom they consulted attributed this to "an excess of electric vitality." The anxious mother forbade the lad any literature that might prove too stimulating, but sensibly gave up when he went to Eton, and only asked that he refrain from Byron.

The diminutive Swinburne survived Eton, having established among his peers that he would fight back like a mouse gone mad, but was carried away by a curious fascination with flogging, which he had witnessed more often than he had endured it. This morbidity might have distressed the father, had he known, but the Lady Henriettas, on the whole, are not conversant with such pleasures. His reckless behaviour did disturb her, as did his early tendency to strong drink.

His landlady also disapproved and when he departed said, "I've had me full of them tiresome Balliol gentlemen."

When he came up to London it was on a very tight rein and a very small allowance, but with the completed manuscripts of two historical dramas. And once ensconced in rooms at 16 Grafton Street, Fitzroy Square, he had found Gabriel and his circle as easily as a honeybee finds heather. One of Gabriel's attractive qualities was a generous pleasure in the gifts of others; ungrudgingly he read and praised *The Queen Mother* and *Rosamund*, and he adopted the elf as a younger brother.

That spring Gabriel happened to be a few pounds in pocket. Old Brown had sold a painting at a pretty profit and for the first time had a bank account and could write cheques; this meant that Gabriel could forget the paltry debt he owed his friend, who was not going to suffer. With this in mind, he wanted to do something for Lizzie that would require Swinburne's help.

Swinburne would have given Gabriel anything he had or that he could raise, but because of the foresight of his father could do neither. He was relieved to find that what Gabriel wanted was only his moral suasion.

"Lizzie has been depressed," Gabriel said. "She writes poems about Deverell."

Walter Deverell, the young man so beautiful that women followed him upon the street, was dead some time. The Brotherhood had eased his last months as best they could and especially his anxiety for his widowed mother and younger brothers and sisters. They had finished his paintings for him, arranged his sales, contributed their own funds to the distressed household, and taken turns sitting by his bed.

And then one day, standing with Lizzie at the window of Chatham Place and looking out over the vast span of the great bridge, Old Brown, startled, had said, "There goes Deverell."

And indeed, in that hour he died.

Certainly Walter Deverell had admired Elizabeth Siddal, although he was never much attracted to the ladies. But Lizzie, brooding over her long spinsterhood, had decided that he had waned for love of her and that she had been cruel. Gabriel recognized in this a blow struck at what she chose to consider his own cruelty to her. It made him uncomfortable and impatient, and besides, he thought her verses mawkish.

"I think of a few weeks by the sea," he said. "Fresh air, long walks, early hours; do her a world of good. But she won't go. Talk it up to her, do, there's a good fellow."

At this Swinburne performed in a fashion that his family felt had stunted his growth. He stretched his arms down his sides and shook his hands so that he resembled an agitated triangle.

He would do what he could, although he was dubious about persuading Lizzie to anything against which she had set her mind. He wanted to see her anyway because he was gleefully working on a ballad of which Gabriel disapproved. Fierce as she was in defense of her own virtue, about other people's Lizzie was not easily shocked.

When she opened the door to him, Swinburne bowed deeply and proclaimed, *"Ave, Faustina Imperatrix!"* And shivering in the dank air he added, *"Morituri te salutamus."*

She laughed her Kent Road laugh that the others seldom heard and said, "Then come in and take off that sodden coat."

For it was April again. Cold mists coiled through the streets and the air was wet and heavy. Lizzie's room was dark; she sat in a low chair leaning to the little light, a drawing on her knees. Ruskin had preferred that she draw directly in colour, but since she was no longer committed to him, she drew as she pleased.

"Put it down, Princess," Swinburne said. "I want to read to you."

And indeed he had for the moment forgotten the object

of his visit, a circumstance almost certain to arise whenever an artist can command an audience. So carried away was the poet with the magnificence of his song that he was slow to notice that Lizzie, who was a good listener, began to look not so much startled as amused.

> Wine and rank poison, milk and blood,
>   Being mixed therein
> Since first the devil threw dice with God
>   For you, Faustine.

Because she was a poet herself she understood his excitement and why his voice squeaked.

> Even he who cast seven devils out
>   Of Magdalene
> Could hardly do as much, I doubt,
>   For you, Faustine.

And she could see why Gabriel disapproved. Some might call Rossetti's poems sensuous, though he would never name them such, but contrary to what Christina thought, he did not blaspheme: he would be afraid to do so. Lizzie was only afraid that she might smile. But now Swinburne went too far.

> What adders came to shed their coats?
>   What coiled obscene
> Small serpents with soft stretching throats
>   Caressed Faustine?

Lizzie threw back her golden head and her laugh shook the sombre room. Cut to the quick, her little friend regarded her in silence; after a moment he spoke icily.

"Why do you laugh?" he asked.

"Why, it is only that you are so — excessive."

She was truly sorry to have offended him, but not so sorry as she was shortly to be. More than most, Lizzie should have remembered how painful it is to have one's efforts underestimated and one's personal habits exaggerated; Swinburne seemed to think that the word "excessive" applied to both.

"And you? And you?" he sputtered. "At least I don't drown myself in laudanum."

Now she was the one offended; nay, lacerated. She knew that Gabriel was much concerned about what he considered her dependence upon that benign drug, and that Swinburne should also know it meant that she had been discussed. It is intolerable to be discussed.

"He sent you," she said angrily. "You are his spy."

Green eyes glared into green. She could not have said anything better designed to enrage him. He, a spy? Swinburne, the libertarian, the scourge of tyrants, who as a boy traveling with his parents refused to return the bow of Louis Napoleon? And had written about it, too.

When the devil's riddle is mastered
And the galley-bench creaks with a Pope,
We shall see Buonaparte the bastard
Kick heels with his throat in a rope . . .

A spy? *He?*

But now, like children fearful of having broken some treasure that cannot be replaced and without which their home, their haven, can never be the same, they looked at one another. Then Swinburne dashed to her and buried his fiery head in her lap.

She bent to him. She said, "Forgive me. I am not well."

"Princess," he said, "I know." And then remembering the purpose of his visit he added, "That is why Gabriel wants you to have this holiday."

She looked down with her heavy eyelids narrowed and then tossed her stubborn little chin.

"He wants me on holiday so that he may frequent Jane Burden."

He was astonished at the perfidy that this uncovered. For if Gabriel wished to see more of Jane Burden than he already did (he met her constantly in the company of his young friends and, for that matter, she sat for him for long hours which no one dared to disturb), he was disloyal not only to Lizzie but to William Morris. To suspect him was perfidious of her.

"Miss Burden," he reminded her, "is engaged to be married to Mr. Morris."

Lizzie rested her head against the back of her chair. In that dull room her hair flamed like a sunset on a threatened evening.

"One may admire," she said, and her voice quivered, "and be admired, even where it is not permitted."

He was wrung with pity, seeing that the condition of women is pitiable; they can only wait to be acted for, or acted against. And then remembering that Elizabeth Siddal did not consider herself one of her own ilk, he was inspired.

"Princess, he says your new poems are remarkable."

One could not say that Lizzie brightened; she may have bridled.

"I have had much time to think on them," she said.

Lizzie's sad-coloured little drawings had been purchased by a friend and praised by strangers, but her poems had never been printed and not many asked to see them. She rose at once and fetched a handful of loose pages filled with close, spidery lines.

Swinburne received them respectfully and Lizzie, leaving him to peruse them, glided ghostlike into her inner room. He sighed slightly and dutifully began to read. They were very melancholy.

> Farewell, Earl Richard,
> Tender and brave!
> Kneeling I kiss
> The dust from thy grave . . .

That, of course, would be Walter Deverell, whom the maiden and poetess now mourned. But while the true knight lived had she been kind? No!

> How sounded my words so still and slow
> To the great strong heart that loved me so?

What a comfort now that Deverell was in his grave! For now Lizzie could openly acknowledge the devotion that honour had once forbidden and that now, nobody could deny. The true poet stirred uncomfortably, not because the lines were morbid (he was himself accused of morbidity), but because they were banal. Furthermore, the lines were not about lost love but false love. In one she spoke as the faithless knight, now racked by a reasonable remorse:

> I live to know that she is gone —
> Gone, gone forever, like the tender dove
> That left the ark alone.

In one, before her own demise, she reproached:

> I can but give a sinking heart
> And weary eyes of pain,
> A faded mouth that cannot smile
> And may not laugh again.

Algernon Charles Swinburne clasped his hands together in a spasm of regret. These poems could not fail to infuriate Gabriel.

Observe the unfair advantage that Lizzie took. Swinburne never addressed real personages, excepting public figures, who are fair game; his lion-limbed women prowled only in antiquity, and if he named a mistress, she was the sea. But Lizzie's false knight was too obviously her affianced, who was not even allowed anger, since she could shrug and claim she toyed with the pretty times of Froissart and of Malory. Then again, though her complaints might stir his pity they could not heat his ardour, and his pity and her pride at the best made cold partners.

When Lizzie rejoined him from the farther room she looked somewhat less attenuated and she smelled, faintly, of brandy; which made Swinburne anxious to get away so that he might get hands on a dram of his own. But what to say before he made his escape? About art one cannot — may not — lie, which makes the evasion of friends so difficult. So Swinburne rolled the papers carefully, put them between her hands, and then placed his hands over hers.

He said, "You are a very lovely woman."

Then of his grief and his affection he burst forth. "Oh Lizzie, cannot you write more *happily?*"

"Not unless Jane Burden marries Morris," she said.

As it happened, Jane Burden did marry William Morris. His devotion was unshakable, her will was his law, and his income was sure and sizable.

And besides, Dante Gabriel Rossetti never asked her.

15

B UT THE SID'S MELANCHOLIA was not as much relieved by the marriage of the Morrises as she had
hoped. Others were marrying, too: Ned Jones had taken
a new name (from an aunt) and a wife (whom he had
found for himself); and even Holy Hunt had replaced
Annie Miller with someone more suitable. None of these
wives had waited for ten years; their men were eager for
them.

Lizzie again sat by herself in Hastings.

She wore once more the old striped silk; the quarters
of artists' women do not accommodate hoopskirts. Number 12 Beach Houses smelled of gutted fish and Mrs.
Chatfield had, at first, leaped to the wrong conclusion
about her boarder's malady. But Lizzie was not pregnant.
She was only too tired to write, too weak to paint, too
sick to walk — and for whom should she write or paint?
Ruskin was no longer interested in his Ida.

John Ruskin was, in fact, less and less interested in
either art or artists, and his fierce intellect had turned

to society — to industry, education, morals, and religion — and he was scolding a new public by means of a series of lectures and pamphlets, some of them so alarming that William Makepeace Thackeray closed the door of *The Cornhill Magazine* to this agitator.

But when Lizzie pressed her fingers to her flaming hair and paced the low room, the walls of which grew closer because in some merry fit Mrs. Chatfield had papered them with nosegays, and while she attempted to conceal her basin and sent down again her empty trays, it was not of John Ruskin that she thought. No, since Janey had married Topsy Morris, Lizzie's grief had not lessened and Gabriel's, she suspected, had increased.

All else went well with him. Even his need of money was not so much to supply want as to supply playthings. Within weeks a Miss Baring commissioned, for fifty pounds, *The Magdalene at the Door of Simon the Pharisee;* Lady Trevelyan, *Mary in the House of John;* and one Mr. Leatheart not only offered but produced three hundred and sixty-seven pounds for the unfinished and ill-fated *Found.* Yet still Gabriel moped and still he put Lizzie off.

She thought, because of a sonnet she had found, that she knew why. His sonnets were shockingly unprivate, and if Brown or Holy Hunt, for instance, grew restless and objected, saying that there were some thoughts and certain feelings that a British gentleman kept to himself, Gabriel would only hoot and say, "Thank God I am not wholly British!"

But he was British enough so that it did not occur to him that anyone, uninvited, would invade the privacy of his papers. So she found and read.

Their bosoms sundered, with the opening start
   Of married flowers to either side outspread
    From the knit stem; yet still their mouths, burnt red,
Fawned on each other where they lay apart.

She was repulsed, as any decent woman would have been. Very well, then, she saw what had happened. But with whom? Because if it were Fanny Cornforth, that - - *creature* — it would be bearable. So she searched feverishly and, with the bad luck of the searcher, found.

> . . . the smooth black stream that makes thy
> whiteness fair . . .

Had Jane Burden, then, been bride to Gabriel before she had been bedded by his friend?

She could not keep the laudanum down and without the laudanum she could not stop the shuddering that racked her frail length, and unless she could stop the shuddering she could not possibly walk the streets that lay between her and more laudanum.

Then why had he not married Janey? Was it because he thought that she, Lizzie, was going to die? Meantime he would not break his vows nor keep them, because if Death were going to cancel their sad contract, he could wait. But Janey would not wait.

Wringing her hands, pacing and tripping in the skirts of the striped silk, Lizzie knew this was not true: he did not wish Elizabeth Siddal dead. Not in his waking mind. But in these ten embittered years since she had been the age that Jane was now — Jane, who was ten when Gabriel first tipped The Sid's face up to his — Lizzie had learned that there are dark things one does wish.

There had been a day when she thought, if Gabriel were to die, no one would look for me to marry.

And so the Night-Mare galloped and the morning came when Mrs. Chatfield, mounting the stairs with the can of hot water, found Lizzie spitting like a cat and hot as coals: this was in earnest.

The Chatfields had not for themselves ever required

the services of a physician, although her sciatica was wicked and his leg, which had been shot off at Waterloo, still walked at night. Chatfield was so much older than his missus that he had almost not proposed at all, but when he asked if she could think of marrying him, she had given him a silent answer; tenderly, she had touched his terminated leg.

The Chatfields had been very happy, and neither of them wanted to see the beautiful young woman so sick and so alone. Mr. Chatfield was compelled to admit what otherwise he might have kept to himself — that when he took Miss Siddal's letters to the pillar-box he had taken note of the address to which she wrote. Because, he said — coming out with it — because they would not want their daughter not to have someone know, not if she needed. Not if they had had a daughter.

"*Chatfield!*" she said.

And there was so much loving approbation in her voice that he thought that after all, perhaps, he had not taken advantage of her.

The letter that Gabriel received said only that Mrs. Chatfield thought he had better come at once if he wished to see his friend alive.

Gabriel's conscience was not of the best; he came immediately, embraced her with his early passion, and undertook the tedious and distressful details of nursing her; and she, who for so long had gone to such lengths to conceal from him the unromantic nature of her malady, did not conceal it now nor have the strength to do so. She lay emaciated, her golden hair damp with sour sweat and her frail body racked with the spasms that prevented her from retaining one morsel of sustenance or one drop of the liquids without which she dried like a mummy.

Rossetti was terrified. He pleaded with her not to leave

him; he could not lose his treasure to the grave. He promised to make good his promise: he vowed to take her back
to Paris as his wife. When he could briefly leave her bedside, he hurried to the stationer and ordered writing paper
for her with the new initials and he prayed that she would
live to see that writing paper. What could he have been
thinking of? To lose wit, genius, beauty? He applied for
a special license in case she was too weak to get to church,
and he held that license up before her eyes.

First she could manage water, a teaspoon at a time,
and at last, by the teaspoon also, broth and jellies. The
day came when he wrote to William Michael that they
would marry, but that before that happened he must return to London for a few days to get some money he had
left in a drawer at Chatham Place.

Then she relapsed.

The doctor said if this could not be prevented, Miss
Siddal would die of starvation and exhaustion; she looked
already like a corpse. Again Gabriel was frantic. Yet
frenzy cannot be maintained, and as if Lizzie recognized
that melancholy fact, she forced herself again. Slowly the
colour seeped into her thin cheeks, once more she held
water down, and at last soup; and on the twenty-second
of May — and to the astonishment of everyone — she left
her bed, dressed, and came downstairs.

The next day there appeared at the parish church in
Hastings, to be married, "Dante Gabriel Rossetti, artist
and bachelor, and Elizabeth Eleanor Siddal, both of full
age." And, as it was recorded, "Said marriage duly witnessed by Alfred and Jane Chatfield, both of that town."
That same afternoon, while the good Mrs. Chatfield helped
the new Mrs. Rossetti with her packing, Gabriel sat down
and took his pen in hand to write to his friend Brown.

"All hail from Lizzie and myself just back from church."
Then he sat in the darkening sitting room moodily chew-

ing on his pen. "I am sorry I cannot give you good news of her health, but we must hope for the best . . ."

It is unfortunate that the inconstant heart sways like a reed in a high breeze; but so it is. Gabriel was almost as exhausted as his spouse, and in no mood for Paris. She had promised to live and he to wed; now it was done and no more to be said. He had heard that Brown was visiting with Jane (the oxen-eyed) and William Morris; he himself was anchored and fast-fettered, and as his pale wife entered in her cloak and bonnet and with her reticule, he sighed.

He wrote: "best love to the Topsies."

Frances Lavinia and the girls did not exactly welcome Lizzie. They did, after due consideration and after much debate, send her a wastebasket.

16

MORRIS, MARSHALL, FAULKNER AND CO.
Fine Art Workmen
In Painting, Carving, Furniture, and the Metals
8 Red Lion Square, Holburn, W.C.

Members of the Firm

F. Madox Brown

C. J. Faulkner

Arthur Hughes

E. Burne-Jones

P. Paul Marshall

W. Morris

D. G. Rossetti

Philip Webb

WILLIAM MORRIS was in his element; the firm was formed and flourishing, and he was building a castle for his lady. He had wished to reform British taste and to marry Janey, and already he had done the one and was well on his way to the other. And since the workrooms at Red Lion Square would not accommodate the orders that poured in, he erected on the Thames the Red House, with deep little windows and vast halls to display his wife's medieval grace.

Janey herself said that she would have preferred something that looked newer and less . . . well, queer. Or so
she was rumoured to have said.

Only a man of tremendous energies could manage so
many temperaments and still contribute the ferment of his
own ideas and the skill of his own hands, but Topsy Morris
was such a man. Spurred by his enthusiasm, the firm
poured forth novelties to titillate and seduce the British
matron.

Will Little's mother was one who was seduced. At first
she had gasped at the luxuriant colours and bold patterns
of the wallpapers, the massive subtle carpets, the painted
ornamentation that covered chests and armoires; then she
bought of them gleefully, as all her friends were doing.
She hesitated only at the solid and simple Morris chair,
with a great back which reclined to any angle — and
that, only because she thought that it might dwarf her
son.

"Your father would have liked it, though," she said.

In his new house, Topsy dressed his wife to comple-
ment her domain. Janey wore heavy fabrics woven abroad
that were cut full and simply, but clung to the lines of her
tall body; they might present a problem in the washing
room but became her brooding presence well. To the Red
House, in the spring of 1861, were summoned the members and friends of the firm to celebrate the birth of a
daughter.

Will Little was relieved to be included. Although he
still saw much of the old friends, including William
Michael, who seemed to invite his opinion and even, sometimes, to brood about it, he was not at all so sure of the
young fellows, neither of whom had asked for his advice.
Topsy Morris had treacherously turned out to be compe-
tent enough to content the most critical and Ned Burne-
Jones did not recognize that he needed aid, bemused as

he was by his gentle Georgiana, who was so kind that she referred to those of dubious virtue only as women whose "goodness was in abeyance."

It was the custom of all of them to gather together, because that was pleasant, and to go down by railway, because that was necessary; then Topsy and his man met you with pony carts. Three miles away or thereabouts was the Red House with its odd high-pitched roof, and the dining hall of baronial height; and there waiting for them, either in blue or red — because so far those were the only colours that Topsy had any luck in dyeing — was silent Janey, smiling.

Gabriel had been high of spirit on the way down from London, although Lizzie did not accompany him. She had miscarried and was carrying again and was very bitter, because at that hard time none of the Rossetti women had come near her. Of Frances Lavinia, in her widowhood, nothing was expected. Maria was deep in her efforts for the Saint Mary Magdalene Home for Fallen Women, on Highgate Hill, and she spoke already about retiring to the convent there.

Christina's life already had become conventlike, as she retreated from sundry disappointments. William Bell Scott wooed her no more, Charles Bagot Cayley was too intimidated to be more than the most faint of friends, and John Ruskin did not like her poems. It happened that Gabriel, feeling that something must be done to cheer his sister, had prevailed again upon the patience of his old friend. Ruskin had replied:

> I sate up till late last night reading the poems. They are full of beauty and power. But no publisher — I am deeply grieved to know this — would take them, so full they are of quaintness and offences.

Mrs. Browning's day had come and gone and Gabriel considered that Christina wrote quite as well as Mrs. Browning. Ruskin, however, did not think so.

> Irregular measure (introduced to my great regret, in its chief wilfulness, by Coleridge) is the calamity of modern poetry . . .

At first Gabriel, who was as devious as the next, had thought not to repeat any of this to her. But none are brutal as poets to those who pretend to be poets. And so he told her of the judgment of John Ruskin:

> Your sister should exercise herself in the severest commonplace of metre until she can write as the public likes.

Gabriel was thirty-two years of age and so was Will Little, though Will's mother said he was fresh-faced as a babe. Georgiana Jones was the youngest of the lot, and she would not see twenty-one again; Will thought it was preposterous the way they all behaved. Ghost stories were bad enough and so were pillow fights, with the ladies in nightgowns that could hardly be distinguished from their daytime wear, and when somebody threw an apple that caught Topsy Morris in the eye and closed it, Will thought it served him right. But when they decided to play hide-and-seek and even Juno picked up her heavy skirts, tossed back the weight of her black, wiry hair, and fled giggling down a long, echoing hall, Will followed soberly, took up his station where an arras masked an open doorway, and prepared to sit it out. The halls were dark, but not even Topsy was so benighted as to have replaced the lamps with torches.

And so Will Little, whose foot had gone to sleep but

who would not budge now, not even if the other foot grew numb, saw perfectly clearly when Gabriel Rossetti caught up with the tall figure — there were only two of the fair who were that tall, and the other was not there — put his hand across her laughing mouth, and then removed it and replaced it with his mouth. They stayed for a long moment like that, her gown, like a dark calla lily, belling about her feet. And then she bent her dusky head and Gabriel buried his face in that harsh dusk.

Later, at the huge T-shaped table where William Morris sat with his great corded arms dyed indigo with woad, Gabriel shook his head when the wine went round. He did not touch his food nor once look at his host nor at his hostess, but only played with a handful of raisins.

Even in that big house, there were so many of them that there was no possibility of beds for everyone. The gentlemen slept upon the floor, except for one. Swinburne was small enough so that a sofa was accorded to him; this did not altogether please Will Little, who thought as he eased gingerly from one hip to the other that the difference in their height was not worth a tittle.

Eventually, they slept. But Will, shocked and excited, turned over and over in his mind what he had seen; in such cases, it is not easy to balance loyalties. Out in the early garden a bird called.

Yes. Like it or not, he must warn Lizzie.

17

LIZZIE WAS BROUGHT to bed of the stillborn child she had almost brought to term. When Gabriel tried to comfort her, she turned her face away.

"This is the second baby you have killed," she said.

Some things are better left unsaid because they will not be forgotten.

Her strength was slow in coming back. She made no effort: would not have her shoulders propped, would not sit up, would not swing her long feet veined with blue over the side of the disordered bed. When the midwife threw up her hands and said that over the way she would be needed any hour, rather than have her husband near her, Lizzie rose. Then she sat on a stool in what passed as their sitting room; the door had been painted apple-green and like the Red House, the walls of Chatham Place were hung with tapestries.

There she sat for days while with a white and flaccid hand she rocked the empty cradle.

Some were touched by this but others were annoyed; even the patient Brown said Lizzie had a turn for histrionics. Ned Burne-Jones was simply frightened. His Georgie was herself anticipating, and he had not thought before to contemplate such a conclusion. He stopped at Chatham Place hoping to find Gabriel, who was not at home; Ned hoped he had not gone to Wapping to visit Fanny Cornforth. To the consternation of his friends, Gabriel spent more and more time in Wapping, seeking Fanny's bawdy cheer and other coarse comforts with which Lizzie did not provide him.

By the cradle Lizzie, her lovely green eyes vacant as glass and her bright hair daft as her manner, raised her finger to her lips.

"Hush, Ned," she said. "You'll wake her."

However, she recovered. One day she rose in a cold rage and gathered together all the soft, small garments over which she had bent so lovingly, and packed the cradle with them.

"Take it to Georgie Jones," she said.

But Gabriel spoke nervously to Ned.

"Lizzie has been talking to me of parting with a certain small wardrobe to you," he said. "But don't let her, please. It looks such a bad omen for us."

Ned moodily agreed, but Georgie did take the cradle and soon laid in it a beautiful and lively child, and in that household there was rejoicing.

Others were also dissatisfied in that sour season, and one of them was Ruskin; even his father asked anxiously for his liver. Ruskin was losing patience with all of the Rossettis. He had promised to advance to Gabriel a hundred pounds to insure the publication of his translations from the Italian, but though *The Early Italian Poets Together with Dante's "Vita Nuova"* was very beautiful, it was also filled with errors, and though he had pointed this out the stubborn Gabriel still meant to publish.

Worse: Christina Rossetti had found a publisher and, although *Goblin Market* was still in manuscript, Ruskin understood that those in the know were greeting it with hysterical approbation. Why, there were those who said she was a genius!

Little wonder that he wrote ruefully to a Professor Charles Eliot Norton of Harvard College in America that he was at present "an entirely puzzled, helpless, and disgusted old gentleman."

And before the birth of the ill-fated child, Lizzie had refused to see him. He knew that he had little knowledge of the mad ways of women, but he did not for a moment believe what Gabriel had told him — that she had been morbidly aware of her grotesque appearance.

So when Gabriel got into all that nastiness about Mr. Plint's estate, Ruskin was not so ready to help as he once would have been. Plint had been far from the only buyer whose money Gabriel had taken and whose commissions he had not fulfilled, but he was the first inconsiderate enough to die and leave his affairs in the hands of men of business. Now they demanded either the promised paintings or the six hundred and eighty guineas, neither of which he could produce, having spent the one and sold the others.

To Gabriel's feverish appeal his erstwhile benefactor replied: ". . . but I hope somebody will soon throw you into prison. We will have the cell made nice, airy, cheery, and tidy and you'll get on with your work gloriously. Love to Ida."

So as her melancholia increased, there was one less friend Elizabeth Siddal could turn to.

But Christina Rossetti had come into her own.

Unwooed she might be, and unwed, but though she had

not yet seen her book between boards, she was to be published, and before her brother. Moreover, her poems were the children of her own mind and not, like his translations, fosterlings.

But these, she knew, were nursery feelings; more deeply, she was reverent that the Creator permits the creature to create. What regal generosity! Therefore when her brother (grown a bit heavy, grown a little tired) came glooming into their small drawing room, she thought only with sympathy of the chains of the flesh he had not been able to break, because he had not listened to his sister's stern ukase: . . . *kneel, wrestle, knock, do violence, pray.*

Meantime the mother, straight-backed, arthritic, and proud, looked critically at her young who, in truth, no longer were so young. Except for William Michael they were all unpredictable. Even Maria. Her daughters thought she had not known, but when Maria had lain night-long across Christina's door lest she rise and go to William Bell Scott, of course the mother had known. Though the mother had suspected then, and did now know, that Christina could have been prevented less dramatically.

It was from that experience, she thought, that Christina had drawn *Goblin Market*, with its soft, sensuous images that glowed and burst with sweetness like the forbidden fruit itself. And she wondered how much mockery there was in the conclusion of that poem which had been so much admired as an encomium to family ties.

> "For there is no friend like a sister,
> In calm or stormy weather,
> To cheer one on the tedious way,
> To fetch one if one goes astray,
> To lift one if one totters down,
> To strengthen whilst one stands."

As if he had caught her thought — so often children do — her elder son inquired, "Maria still parades around in that habit?"

Christina's eyes gleamed dangerously. "There is need for her services. So many unhappy women think to flout the will of God."

The mother said quietly, "Christina also helps at the convent."

Gabriel raised his brows. He said, "I should not think Christina had the time to spare."

This could have been a graceful reference to her literary labours, but Christina suspected — and was right — that Gabriel thought her self-centred. But now he spoke of more important things.

"I had been hoping to find William here."

Christina said, "I rather thought so."

This was not kind. It implied that Gabriel would not have come only to see his mother, aged and worthy though she be, nor his sisters, but that he wished to put the touch to William Michael. Again.

Their mother said, "He is often at the Browns' these days. I believed he is very fond of little Lucy."

Lucy Brown was now a grown girl. Brother and sister were drawn close by alarm; if William Michael married, there would be new demands upon his time, his patience, and his income.

Christina felt a sudden sympathy with her brother; the skin below his eyes was stained with fatigue. She said gently, "I hope that Lizzie improves."

"She is stronger but she remains unsteady — and then, she is too much alone."

Both women knew this as reproach, but would not rise to it. That the son and brother had too late married a young woman of questionable reputation did not change the fact that, even had Lizzie come to the marriage with propriety and a portion, they would still not have liked her.

"Perhaps you should be more at home with her yourself?"

Gabriel looked up indignantly. They could not know of Wapping; no gentleman of his acquaintance would mention Fanny to them. How could he be more at home with Lizzie than he was?

"I must work," he said, "and Lizzie does not care for the company of my model. Besides, Swinburne is much with her, and he is lively fare."

Christina blushed hotly; not that she thought that Swinburne might be dangerous to Lizzie's peace of mind, but because he troubled her own. The little man was an atheist, a sensualist, and a drunkard, but he was a glorious poet. She had blotted the most offensive passages with pasted strips but still she read and was mortified to read.

> Wilt thou yet take all, Galilean? but these thou
>   shalt not take,
> The laurel, the palms and the paean, the breasts
>   of the nymphs in the brake . . .

Could one capable of such lines be a fit companion for Rossetti's wife?

Suddenly Gabriel cried out, tormented, "I don't know what to do for Lizzie!"

So Christina withdrew, but not before she put her cold hand briefly upon her brother's brow. Closeted alone she still heard that cry, and she remembered the arrogant and confident youth of a decade before, untested and unafraid. What had happened?

Time.

Now she leaned proudly to her pen, the key to her own liberty, and wrote:

One face looks out from all his canvases,
   One selfsame figure sits or walks or leans:
   We found her hidden just behind those screens,
That mirror gave back all her loveliness.
A queen in opal or in ruby dress,
   A nameless girl in freshest summer-greens,
   A saint, an angel — every canvas means
The same one meaning, neither more nor less.
He feeds upon her face by day and night,
   And she with true kind eyes looks back on him,
Fair as the moon and joyful as the light:
   Not wan with waiting, not with sorrow dim;
Not as she is, but was when hope shone bright;
   Not as she is, but as she fills his dream.

And then she put her head down on her arms and for a
time she wept for him, and for herself and for her parents,
and for Elizabeth Siddal, and for all those who have been
young and beautiful and must relinquish.

18

Lizzie had been very well that morning and even gay.

Gabriel's affairs flourished. By some juggling he had been able to fob off on Plint's executors the paintings promised to other people and, moreover, to extract from those other people sufficient funds to begin new work which would, he vowed, eventually content them.

He had bought Lizzie a new mantle, with which she was pleased.

That winter everyone had been at her to take a holiday and twice, her husband had insisted. He had himself been from home both times and not at ease to think of Lizzie alone at Chatham Place, with the fogs rising from the wintry river and the cold halls echoing at night.

First she had gone to the Red House and then to Emma Brown; both times she had departed in stealth and haste. Since there was no question that Topsy would permit her to contribute in any way to his growing household, Gabriel

had not provided her with funds and, informed of her precipitate departure, had to appeal to his mother.

". . . I know there was not a halfpenny of money at
Chatham Place. If at all possible, would you go there, and
take her some few pounds, which I shall be able to repay
you on my return immediately and will punctually do so?"
It must have been obvious, even to Gabriel, that the old
lady might be reluctant, for he continued, "If not convenient to call, you might send the tin by post."

It may be that the Red House, where Janey Morris presided, was not the wisest place for Gabriel to deposit Lizzie.
But she would not stay with the Browns in Kentish Town
either, but left with such lack of courtesy that the unhappy
Gabriel apologized to his friend.

"She tells me," he wrote, "she felt unwell after you left
yesterday, and finding the noise rather too much for her,
left before your return lest she should be feeling worse."
Since this did not seem to suffice, he added gloomily, "I
write this word since her departure must have surprised
you, as her return did me."

It is perhaps dispiriting to be in the company of a wife
given to dark remarks. "All people who are at all happy or
useful seem to be taken away," said Lizzie.

Her verses remained sombre, too.

> And, mother dear, when the big tears fall
> And the pale church grass waves,
> Then carry me through the dim twilight
> And hide me among the graves.

"Bosh!" Gabriel said when he read this — but only to
himself. For though he found the picture of the burdened
parent comic, it was a long time since Lizzie and he had
laughed together; he held his peace and slipped away to
Wapping.

But with the dirge of the old year done, things grew better. Dame Nature is a severe taskmistress and insists that in her rigorous games one must participate or depart. The coral and then the rose crept back to Lizzie's cheeks. Her shoulders straightened and one day she laughed aloud. Gabriel brightened and began to draw from her again.

Then came a February morning when the early sun dazzled the riverbed; Lizzie leaned from the window and heard the little mudlarks shout at their work as they retrieved the treasures that the mud gave up: bottles and scraps of iron and curios from the pockets of the drowned. Their sacks grew heavy and their hearts grew glad. And so, before the morning passed, did Lizzie's heart grow glad. Because in her presence, Gabriel sent Fanny away, with his arm around that plentitude and such a hug as no reasonable wife could mind.

"Be off with you," he said. "I won't be needing you again, for now."

That meant he was again abandoning *Found*. Fanny had changed and thickened since he began the painting. But with Annie Miller gone, he would always need that broad, common, and lovely face and the torrent of unkempt yellow hair whenever he went back to the fallen country girl. Years can be painted out.

"That's all very well, Rizzetty," Fanny said, and she bobbed politely at his wife. "But don't be sending for me then, for — begging your pardon, ma'am — I've other fish to fry."

"Never fear." He turned on Lizzie his long artist's look. "I need my wife."

He would call it *Regina Cordium*. The Queen of Hearts.

Oh, if husbands knew how easily the poor hearts are assuaged, how soon the frightened, fluttering wings will quiet under a tender hand; how she, the crown of whose existence is his love, needs only to be assured of her treasure to fill his home with her happiness!

Once again at Chatham Place there was merriment and company. Old friends and new friends came, blokes and coves summoned by Gabriel to partake of "oysters and obloquy"; George Meredith — young, ambitious, and embittered — and his friend Hardman, and Swinburne, of course, who shocked both those gentlemen by his prancing and his praise of the Marquis de Sade. And Old Brown came and Morris, when he was in town, and Ned Jones and William Michael; only Holman Hunt, who disapproved of all of them, stayed away. He spoke of Lizzie yet as "that large-throated, disagreeable woman whom he paints."

But over all, beautiful in her pride and holding her head high above the white tower of her throat, Lizzie was enthroned. The Queen of Hearts.

Upon the evening of February tenth, Gabriel, Lizzie (in her new mantle), and Swinburne were to go to dinner. They chose the Sablonnière in Leicester Square. When Swinburne came by in a hansom cab to pick up Lizzie (Gabriel would join them later, as he could), he was disturbed to find her flushed and incoherent.

Lizzie had done a curious thing in the last several months; she had hung the room where she sat with wicker cages, in which she cherished chaffinches, bullfinches, doves; this in despite of Gabriel's loathing, and even fear, of birds. One chaffinch in particular aroused his ire because, although it was so tame that it was Lizzie's custom to let it freely fly about, it was terrified of Gabriel and would, when he entered, beat its wings frantically, emit a tiny squawking, and scrabble back into its cage.

Today that bird was gone and Lizzie paced, her hands knotted at her sides.

"Gabriel opened the window and let it out. He must have," she said darkly.

"Never!" Swinburne cried, astonished.

"You do not know him as I know him. He is cruel. Yes, cruel!"

Uneasily, Swinburne assumed that she had taken brandy; many ladies do if they feel faint or have the megrims, and he knew well — better than most — that some are easily affected by strong drink; and Lizzie was upset about her little bird. But as they descended to the street he kept his hand firmly at her elbow and, once in the cab, he brimmed with wrath to think that anyone at the restaurant might criticize her, and he phrased hot answers in his mind.

"It is impossible," he would begin, "that even the reptile rancour, the omnivorous malignity of Iago himself [he thought that part was rather good] could have dreamed of trying to cast a slur on . . ." Whom? "That incomparable lady whose maiden name was Siddal . . ."

Thus would he refute them.

Then he remembered that no one at the Sablonnière was likely to attack Lizzie except Gabriel himself. Nervously, he glanced sideways. Her cheeks were bright, but a lock of her red-gold hair hung loose and willful, and her gloved fingers fidgeted in her lap.

"Princess," he said. "You are quite certain you are up to this? If you choose not to come, I could explain to Gabriel."

She turned upon him the long, cold, steely Kent Road look.

"Whatever are you talking about?" she said.

What crept to his nostrils in the enclosed cab was not only brandy but also the faint, familiar, sickening smell of laudanum.

Unfortunately, Gabriel was very late. Swinburne, listening to her disjointed speech and seeing the light dulled in her long, green eyes, himself attracted the interest of those about them. He suffered one of his conspicuous spasms: his arms twitched, his hands fluttered, the fiery aureole of his hair trembled about his small, white face. What an ob-

server could not know is that within him every vein and
organ shook and jumped. Such sufferers will, in despite of
the opinion of others, snatch at any anodyne, and Swinburne ordered wine.

When Gabriel arrived he found them both with glasses
before them.

If you had asked him, Gabriel would have said that in
the commonwealth of artists, each is self-enfranchised. But
then, he did not really think of Lizzie as an artist. And she
was a woman. He had allowed her — and indeed encouraged — some latitude in her behaviour, because it was convenient for him; but in his heart he honoured the gentlewomen of his own family, with their iron control. None of
them would have chosen to appear in a public restaurant.
No one of them, outside the fortress of her own home,
would have accepted a glass of wine. All would have been
appalled to be seen with a gentleman who was tipsy.

And Lizzie was disheveled; her conversation veered from
reproach to raillery; she had little to say to her husband,
but leaned solicitously to her playmate, fondly scolding
him.

"Is he not wicked?" she demanded archly. "What would
the Admiral say?"

Embarrassment is eased by anger. Gabriel's pulse was
fast and his voice rose as he attempted by his own aplomb
to indicate that there was nothing here to warrant the interest of strangers.

Unfortunately, not everybody was a stranger.

The Sablonnière was fairly new and much frequented by
their friends, who were always in search of a meeting place
removed from the din of the nurseries. But he who stood in
the doorway was one whose expectations had not been soft-
ened by a nursery, and who had little love for Lizzie at any
time, and who, in short, was Will Little.

"Damn it to hell," said Gabriel.

The last time they had met together, Will had made a conspicuous exit from Chatham Place when Swinburne had removed his clothes and danced. Gabriel had been amused and not offended by his departure, but Will could not know this. And since there is no bitterness like that of an old friend and no tongue as devastating, Will was the last person by whom Gabriel wanted to be seen in the company of an inebriated poet and an agitated wife.

Will paused, smiled, and began resolutely to thread through tables toward them.

"Smuggery!" Swinburne said.

At which Will wheeled as easily as a skater and pretending neither to have seen nor heard, glided away from them.

And Lizzie laughed aloud.

The waiter hovered. Gabriel said, "Lizzie, we are going home."

She rose at once, but as she did so, over went her glass, and her thin hand flew to her throat as the red wine soaked into the folds of the new mantle as if it were blood.

They said nothing to one another on the way home and she wondered if there would be anything, ever, to say again. Her conscience was oppressed for leaving a friend so vulnerable, when she well knew Swinburne was not equipped to exercise discretion: more than once when he was leaving Chatham Place, Lizzie had pinned to his coat a paper bearing his address. And worse: following her husband up the stairs to their rooms above the fetid river, she felt her heart drumming in an exquisite agony and her body so weakened that she doubted that she could lift one foot above the other. She dragged her bonnet from her head and dropped the ruined mantle on the bed. What, only since this morning, had happened to her New Found-land?

But Lizzie knew. Having survived disease, delay, and disappointment, she was brought to earth by a pebble no larger than that which had brought down Goliath. That, too, had sufficed.

There had arrived that very morning from a Miss Heaton of Leeds a letter and an emolument which had been the very occasion of this woeful celebration. There was nothing about Miss Heaton to trouble Lizzie; she was a lady of a certain age. But the painting in which Miss Heaton now rejoiced, Gabriel had called *Regina Cordium*.

Lizzie was not at all the Queen of Hearts.

He would not stay more than a moment in the same room with her, but she heard him pace beyond the door, and as she sank to her dressing table she was shaken with welcome anger. He had not been true to her through the years, nor overly kind. He had allowed her to risk her name and he had used her money. He had persuaded her that she, like him, had gifts, and now he called her drawings amateurish and her verses twaddle. He had not, since they married, protected or defended her or loved her.

This very night he had not prevented her from exposing herself to the interest of her inferiors; from such interest there is no recovery. Lizzie reached, at first with no question and then in panic, for her laudanum. It was gone.

She burst through the door like Morgan le Fay, her eyes wild, her hair a bright, floating web. He was shrugging into his greatcoat.

"You took my medicine!" she cried.

He said, "I took your drugs."

"But I must have it," she said. "I will go mad."

"I think you have gone mad."

His eyes were black with rancour. He turned, and as he turned she said, "Where are you going? You are not going out!"

He sighed with a cold patience. "I am going to the college. It is my night."

"It is not your night. You are going to that slut."

"At least," he said, "Fanny is pleasant company."

It was this kind of anger and this kind of neglect that had killed her child.

She said, "With this kind of neglect you killed our child."

He made no move to strike her. Rather, he put his hand into his pocket and withdrew the vial.

"Here," he said. "Take what you like. Why don't you take it all?"

How could a moment, a mere word, be irreparable? And she saw, not the haggard man, but the boy who had loosed her golden hair and crowned her with wildflowers.

"I implore you, Gabriel," she said. "Do not leave me."

"Lizzie," he said — and somehow his words were the worse because his voice was not ungentle — "this is intolerable."

"But it's been better," she begged. "It's been better for some time. I have felt better — haven't I been better?"

Fatigue circled the bright Italian eyes. But he was silent. He meant that, for him, nothing had been better.

She had cost him a lot. He had cost her, too. It had never been any different, not from the beginning.

"Don't go," she said. "I warn you."

He smiled; the apple-green door closed behind him. And Lizzie Siddal stood with the full vial in her hand.

Mrs. MacIntyre, who was not the landlady but as close to one as the owners were like to find, said at the inquest that the Rossettis got along, far as she knew, well as any married couple.

Mr. Rossetti had been from home and had returned at about eleven-thirty. He had come pounding down the stairs and begged her to go to his wife while he fetched a doctor.

The poor lady was breathing most peculiar and was quite unconscious; her pretty face was a dark ugly colour.

Dr. Hutchinson had used the stomach pump but lor! you could tell he had no hope. Mrs. Rossetti had told Mrs. MacIntyre that she had taken quarts of laudanum in her day. No, Mr. Rossetti had not stayed the whole time; at about five in the morning he had went to fetch his friend Mr. Brown.

The magistrate always suspected foul play in that part of town, particularly now that there were those who wrote and painted there: who knows what next? But he could elicit nothing from Mrs. MacIntyre, who had not thought it strange that the husband should leave the bedside; no, nor that later he would not approach the coffin of his wife. The poor man. And then, perhaps Mrs. MacIntyre did not wish to discuss that she herself had tucked beneath the cadaver's narrow feet the light, hard body of the little bird; frozen to death, it had, upon the outside windowsill.

Dr. Hutchinson said there was no doubt in his mind; the room reeked of laudanum — and then, there was the empty vial. Dr. John Marshall, summoned at six, agreed, though neither cared to guess whether it happened by accident or design.

Mr. Swinburne made a bad witness. He talked too much, though he insisted that the deceased had been in the best of spirits; even beyond her wont.

Ford Madox Brown said nothing that he could not avoid. He was much afraid of a verdict of felo-de-se. By the act of 1823 it was still commanded that the body of a suicide be interred within twenty-four hours of the verdict, between the hours of nine and twelve at night and without Christian rites of sepulture; now he feared the effect of such harsh proceedings upon the fevered imagination of his friend.

And more. Brown was Protestant, as far as he was anything. But Gabriel, whether he remembered it or not, was Catholic: had he cost Lizzie her immortal soul?

Therefore Brown did not mention, though he dared not destroy, the scrap of paper to which he had bent where it lay half hidden beneath the flung coverings of the disordered bed.

"My life is so miserable I wish for no more of it," she had said.

They were all cockneys, neighbours, poor; they knew well enough what people are pushed to and how husband and wife can quarrel bitterly and mean no harm, winter-pinched and fearful of the bailiff, of the icy drafts along the rotting floors, of that cough that never did let up.

Their verdict was that the lady had died "accidentally, casually, and by misfortune."

God save us from the same.

II

Janey

19

Oh, who knows the truth?
How she perished in her youth,
And like a queen went down
Pale in her royal gown.

A YEAR LATER Christina wrote those lines, though
she would never say whom, if anyone, she had in
mind. But if she meant Elizabeth Siddal, she erred, for
the reign of that sad queen was just beginning.

Over Tudor House, 16 Cheyne Walk, Chelsea, Fanny
Cornforth presided, though only in the daytime, as housekeeper and model, cook and comforter. At nighttime she
went home to 36 Royal Avenue, where Gabriel installed
her with her drunken husband, who was pleasant as he
could be.

Tudor House suited Gabriel well; rumoured to have been
the residence of Catherine Parr, it is certain that the old

house had served as a pattern for William Makepeace Thackeray, who in *Henry Esmond* had placed the Dowager Viscountess Castlewood there. These romantic associations soothed, and Gabriel felt he could live there alone.

It was not so at first. When he first took the lease of the ancient house with the great garden, friends tried to lighten his hours by living there with him, but though he was desperately lonely, he was unable to use company. What he craved, as Lizzie had craved laudanum, was distraction. He worked like one who flies from fiends, and as a result he prospered and could afford to keep a zoo. In the big, ragged garden on the banks of the Thames peacocks dragged their shimmering trains; he had an Irish deerhound, hedgehogs, dormice, kangaroos. There was an armadillo and a zebra and an ox — because, he said, its eyes were like Janey's. Little furry wombats gamboled indoors and out, but amusing as they were, not everybody liked them. A lady sitting for her portrait objected when one ate her hat.

"Poor thing," said Gabriel. "It will be indigestible."

He bought toys: blue china, candlesticks, crucifixes, objects of faience, brass, and leather that brought him temporary relief. But most of all, he needed voices.

Swinburne moved in with him but proved too distracting. His habits were as unusual as Gabriel's own but more public, and guests were made uneasy by his declamations and by his drunken dances. He slid mother-naked down the banister. Still, he had loved Lizzie, and would not have consented to live with her widower had he considered Gabriel a murderer.

"But I should not have left her on that night," Gabriel said to William Michael. "It was cruel, it was blind, it was selfish."

William Michael's lips tightened. Although he knew it to be unkind, he could not rid himself of the notion that Lizzie had died of pique.

"And I did not appreciate her."

It is astonishing how many, among those who have gone before, were not appreciated while there still was time. "I found this jewel among her papers." And in his rich, musical voice, Gabriel read:

> Holy Death is waiting for me —
> Lord, may I come today?

"And this."

> How is it in the unknown land?
> Do the dead wander hand in hand?

"She would have been another Aspasia," Gabriel said.

To William Michael the lines seemed more indicative of a sickly mind than of great capabilities. Could his brother be serious? Could he who had written of the Blessed Damozel and saw souls like thin flames mount up to God and heard "Time like a pulse shake fierce" really admire this doggerel?

"I shall never write a line again," Gabriel vowed.

William Michael could only hope he would be false to his promise. He was one of many who thought his brother's poetry as beautiful as his paintings, and already there had been great loss, for Gabriel's solitary copies existed only in the faulty memories of his friends.

The Blessed Damozel lay in the grave with Lizzie.

Upon the morning of the funeral and just before the casket was closed Gabriel, who had refused to look upon his dead wife or even to enter the room where she lay did enter there, and with averted eyes he slipped the book that held his manuscript between her white cheek and the riot of her golden hair.

Many had thought the gesture excessive; Ford Madox

Brown, for one, who held nothing in the world more holy than an artist's work, felt it an hysterical penance. William Michael silently agreed. He had said little about it then and nothing now: what was done was done. He pulled out his pocket watch and snapped its cover open; he must be on his way. For William Michael, though he paid for quarters under the towering roof of Tudor House, seldom slept there; nor did George Meredith, who was for a brief time an unlikely tenant.

Gabriel knew the novelist first through a painting called *The Death of Chatterton.* In the picture the Bristol youth of genius lies upon his cot, his soft hair falling loosely, his beautiful face wan, his hand hanging to the empty poison bottle. The face is Meredith's! At seventeen he may have felt a kinship with the poet whom Wordsworth had called "the marvellous boy, the sleepless soul that perished in his pride."

But unlike the marvelous boy, Meredith had lived to become a bitter man to whom Gabriel mistakenly felt akin because Meredith had been cuckolded by a wife who had turned to the arms of his friend as Lizzie had turned to the arms of easeful Death.

Even more interesting: the faithless wife was the daughter of Thomas Love Peacock, intimate friend of Percy Bysshe Shelley, and anyone who had known anyone who had known Shelley had a fast hold on Gabriel's imagination. But they were not fitted to be housemates.

Rossetti was only innocently cruel; impatient he might be, and blind — but never vengeful. Meredith, on the other hand, never had permitted the errant wife to look upon her child again. There was also a strange incident that occurred in the year that little Arthur was six and alternately bullied and indulged. The company was good that day, the wine red, the laughter loud. The lad tugged at his father's sleeve.

"Papa, I want some wine."

Meredith bent to him the full, soft beard that masked his handsome face. "Wine is for gentlemen," he said.

"But why, Papa?"

"Because I say so."

But the little boy had learned that little was forbidden him as long as he did not ask for his Mama. Even Miss Grange, whom Papa said had no sex, could only gently urge her wishes on him but not enforce.

"But Papa, *why?*"

His father's face darkened; he did not like to see the eyes of his guests slide and drop before the prospect of a disobedient son. Arthur's angelic mouth pouted and he tugged again.

"But I want some."

Meredith tossed his splendid head. "Ah," he said, "then you shall have some. And you shall drink it, too."

And he filled not a wineglass but a tumbler, and scowled and forced the child to drink it all. Gabriel would not have done that to a son. If he had had a son.

Yes, the child lived, though he went into coma and was ill for days.

Then too, George Meredith, the son and grandson of a tailor, was jealous to be thought a gentleman, while Rossetti and Swinburne were not. Meredith resented their rough-and-tumble intimacies, their jovial disorder, their table fare and their table manners. Gabriel had once splashed gravy into the face of James McNeill Whistler. There came a morning when Gabriel came growling from his lair.

Meredith said to him, "You are behind on your share of the rent."

The matinal hours were never Gabriel's best. "If you say that again," he said, "I'll throw this teacup in your face."

Meredith touched his bearded lips delicately with his napkin. "But it is true. You're behind with the rent."

So Gabriel threw the teacup (but the tea was not very hot), and Meredith went to his room and gathered his possessions. Thus departed from Tudor House the author of *The Ordeal of Richard Feverel*.

Fanny was a good sort.

She knew that many criticized Rossetti for having her right there in the house, but when his friends came or his family, she stayed out of sight. The place was too big, there was much to do, and someone had to do it. No?

"Besides, Rizzetty," she said, "who else do you know would clean up after wombats?"

Or feed the peahens and the parrots and all them birds she called the chicking?

And she threw back her big head, on which the strong hair sprang glossy as cornsilk, and laughed.

Some thought that Fanny feathered her nest at Gabriel's expense, but there weren't that many feathers floating loose, and if she did pick up a thing or two — well, somebody has to look out for a girl. Who else would shop and clean and cook and try to look out for his awful clothes? Who else had loved him first, before either of those women?

"If you don't get rid of that old velvet jacket," she would threaten, "I'll use it for a bed for the wallaby. She's expecting."

"No you won't," he would say absently. "A good old Elephant wouldn't do so."

He had taken to calling her the Elephant; well, she was fleshy. But he still liked to paint her and she still liked to pose because the pictures came out beautiful and it was restful lolling there. Fanny was lazy and the first to admit.

William Michael minded her most. One day he said,

"I shouldn't think Mr. Hughes would like it — your being away from home so much."

"Oh," she said easily, "Hughes don't mind."

Nor did he. "I give you one thing, Fanny," he would say. "You always make me laugh."

One of the things he thought was funny was the scraps of paper she was always bringing home, under her apron, in her pocket, in her workbag. Studies, Rossetti called them, and not worth much now but might be later. Hughes teased her that she never tired of her own face; well, so she didn't, but that wasn't why the drawings were all of her, Fanny — it was because that sort of made them hers. She was an honest woman, mostly.

When he was working, Rossetti seemed happier. Not happy, but happier. Nowadays he didn't paint the ones Fanny used to like — knights and ladies and horses all carrying on and telling a whole story, every one. Now it was all big single ladies with fat throats and lots of flowers and fur. But they sold well and brought good money.

"Look at it this way, Rizzetty," Fanny told him. "Why not, if that's what they want?"

She thought the ones of her were a lot prettier than the ones of Mrs. Morris. The ones of her were pink and creamy and like a peach about to burst its skin, but the ones of Mrs. Morris had pouty mouths and sad, stern looks under all that black, heavy hair.

There was one painting that Fanny downright didn't like. Rossetti did it of his wife the year after she died and called it *Beata Beatrix*, but it was his wife, all right. In this one she sat all alone, her head was thrown way back and her eyes were closed and a bird nestled in her cupped hands. Fanny hated birds.

What's more, Rossetti didn't like birds either, so why paint one and then look at it day and night? He wouldn't sell that picture, though he had good offers, and he wouldn't put it away, and he kept out all his wife's own sad little paintings too, with those stiff, strange folk that looked as if they had just seen a ghost. It wasn't wholesome.

Something else: Rossetti wasn't sleeping and in the mornings, Fanny saw the signs of it — candles burnt down, books out of place, whiskey bottles, though he had never been what you would call a drinking man, and his face when he at last wandered down would be drawn and sallow.

"Make that room cheerier," Fanny suggested.

Gabriel thought it helped to keep his bedchamber dark as a cave, hung with black draperies and airless as it was lightless and heavily carpeted to keep him from hearing his own footsteps.

"And get up earlier," she scolded. "Walk. Get the air. Lots of people have trouble getting to sleep."

"I'll wager you don't, Fanny," he said.

"Not unless there's something funner to do," she said.

He laughed. She could always make him laugh.

But it got so nights she hated to leave him there alone. Madcap as Swinburne had been, it had been better before Mr. Swinburne's family came down on him and whipped him off into the country, though to be sure he had not been behaving well, but capering about and having fits. Rossetti said he had been provoked. He had brought out a book of poems and people said mean things about it.

One paper had said he had "a mind all aflame with the feverish carnality of a schoolboy," and called poor Mr. Swinburne "an unclean, fiery imp from the pit."

"What do you think of that?" Rossetti brooded. He seemed to think it might rub off on him.

Fanny said, "Sticks and stones may break my bones but names will never hurt me."

Still, it was a shame the little man acted up so odd,

because he had been company and might have helped to take Rossetti's mind off what was happening: his eyes were going bad.

Fanny had burst into his studio as mad as Tophet. He had painted her as Lilith, all soft and rosy, and was going to get a pretty price — though he didn't know she knew it; now it so happens he had promised he would give her half. Oh, there was no way she could hold him to it legal. But there were ways that she could make him smart.

She stopped so short that her skirts whirled around her big thighs. He was not at the easel, but slouched in a chair with his back to the clear north light and his hands gripped as if something hurt. Lately he had been suffering from a hydrocele and more than once the morbid liquid had to be painfully withdrawn.

She said, "What's up, Rizzetty?"

A good fight is fun but only with a laughing, stubborn play-fellow; there is no pleasure in it if your friend is troubled. Not if you love him.

He said, "Fanny. I can't see."

"What do you mean, you can't see?" She sounded ill-tempered, the way you do when something frightens you.

He drummed his fists against his chair and said impatiently, as if she had accused him of something sly, "Everything blurred. Then it went grey. Then it was gone."

"Has it happened before?"

"Yes," he said.

Fanny closed her cornflower eyes and snapped them wide again. She knew that Gabriel's father had died blind, but the old man already had written all his books and had his wife to care for him. Rossetti didn't have a soul except Fanny. And she didn't count.

"You've been using of them too much," she said. "They're just another part of a person and get tired."

And suddenly this arrogant and willful man, this man

whose name was in the papers and whom everybody knew, buckled before her like a child.

"Fanny, don't leave me alone tonight."

She thought of Hughes waiting comfortable for her at home with a glass of grog and a nice chop and a chuckle or two and no ghosts. She thought too of the vase — Etruscan was what Gabriel called it — that was tucked beneath her cloak. She wasn't stealing it — not she — but meant to borrow it for a bit; the "uncle" around the corner had promised the loan of a guinea.

But he looked up to her with those big, dark eyes as if he were the babe she'd never had; no, nor wanted.

So she shrugged the cloak from her shoulders and let it drop and the vase went rolling across the floor and didn't break. He didn't notice, not with his face pressed into the softness and the heat of her. She rocked him back and forth in her big arms.

"There, love," she crooned. "There, dear love, Fanny will stay."

She stayed for a long, long time.

After the baggage moved in bag and baggage, his mother and sisters, who had not often called before, could not call at all. His brother fumed, not so much because he knew her to be common as because he believed her to be dishonest.

"Ah, poor Fanny," Gabriel said. "She does the best she can."

Then he raked his brother with dark, angry eyes, and William Michael did not speak of it again.

And Fanny did ease Gabriel. When his courage failed with the failing light and the vast house filled with shadows and afterthoughts, it was good to have her cheerful vulgarity across the table, her street wisdom and her generous cynicism. Above all, when he started from his sleep, it helped to hear her heavy, healthy breath and to drive phantoms off with the touch of her warm flesh.

She could do nothing about his fear of blindness; it sprang logically from his guilt. Much is excused artists. Because they create what others cannot create, they are permitted to be cruel and indifferent; what is intolerable in others is excused the artist. But if Gabriel were no longer to be an artist? Thus would he be punished.

William Bell Scott urged him to seek the counsel of a physician, but Gabriel was afraid to have his fears confirmed. At last to the dimmed vision and the dizziness pain was added, and one evening he discovered that the faint light of a swaying streetlamp assailed his eyes like the glare of noon. Then he sought counsel.

Sir William Bowman told him to stop work for a month and to take cold-water baths. Bader, the German specialist at Guy's Hospital, agreed, as did a man named Critchett and his own Dr. Hake. They all recommended long walks against the insomnia and they were as one in thinking his difficulty not organic, but the result of overworked, overstrained, and abused nerves.

None of it helped. Nothing helped at all until, tall as a sombre queen, Janey Morris returned again to London.

20

OH, *love!*

We speak now of that unseemly emotion which is quite rightly so embarrassing to the rest of us that we can only countenance it in the young and with laughter — though it must be tolerated, being so unmistakably a part of Nature's war against us all. Let us then recognize in that temporary frenzy a power as much beyond control as are the seasons or the tides, hope that the object is apppropriate, permit — nay, insist — that society sanction the aberration by some formal recognition, and then get back to business.

Love among older people is intolerable, as unbecoming as the whooping cough and as dangerous. We do not mean those sober contracts entered upon by widows and widowers, say, who are in need of aid in their domestic arrangements; in these cases society can only be the better if the contracting parties are comfortable with one another.

But in those past the age of necessity, passion is gro-

tesque and may lead to fornication and adultery and other
such high crimes against the state — for the commission
of which even artists are not forgiven.

So says Will Little.

There are some, however, who do not agree, and one of
them was Dante Gabriel Rossetti.

Fanny Cornforth had a ragamuffin pride and a great
sense of justice. Since she had never permitted Hughes to
be possessive about her or critical of her actions, she could
not in all fairness allow herself to be jealous when Mrs.
Morris became a constant caller at Cheyne Walk — although this does not mean she liked it.

The Firm was doing too well to confine itself to the
Red House and William Morris had had to look for more
commodious quarters. He had advertised that he was able
to supply "any species of decoration, mural or otherwise
from pictures down to the consideration of the smallest
work susceptible of art beauty." It was a cheerful surprise
that so many were susceptible to art beauty.

"I hope you won't be disappointed?" Topsy asked.

"Not at all," said his wife.

Becoming as it was to her, she had never really cared
for the Red House. It was too far from town and she was
seldom able to see her friends; in spite of her spectacular
appearance, Janey Morris was the kind of woman who
liked a gossip and a cup of tea. When they did entertain,
their guests had to be put up for an indefinite term of
time, and Janey did not find this entertaining.

Her husband adored her, but while it was not possible
to overestimate her beauty, it is probable that he did overestimate her capacity to amuse herself; moreover, he was
a man of many parts and many interests which increasingly did not include her. His passionate participation in
the creation of church decoration, metal and glasswares,

handwrought jewelry, wallpapers, printed cottons, and woven tapestries had not, for instance, diminished his interest in poetry, and he had just begun a long manuscript which had nothing to do with her.

Once he had celebrated her, Janey, in his song:

> My lady seems of ivory
> Forehead, straight nose, and cheeks that be
> Hollow'd a little mournfully.
> > *Beata mea Domina!*
> Her forehead, overshadow'd much
> By bows of hair, has a wave such
> As God was good to make for me.
> > *Beata mea Domina!*

That poem had gone on for ninety lines — but then, he had always been prolific. Still and all, it had been more pleasant reading for her than was *The Earthly Paradise*, in which he wrote about the long ago and called himself "the idle singer of an empty day."

Idle, indeed! It may have been that William Morris would have been the better husband had he been more the idle singer and less the businessman, philosopher, and reformer, and it may be the wiser husband had he attended his own early words:

> Her great eyes, standing far apart,
> Draw up some memory from her heart,
> And gaze out very mournfully . . .

> So beautiful and kind they are,
> But most times looking out afar,
> Waiting for something, not for me.
> > *Beata mea Domina!*

But it is not the habit of busy men to linger long over the mournful beauty of their wives' eyes, and perhaps Janey Morris missed his early ardours and regretted that the adoring Topsy, with his mop of fierce curls, his playfulness, his bouts of wild humour, had hardened into this preoccupied man of affairs.

"Have you noticed," Gabriel said one afternoon, "that for all his devotion to the needy classes, he has never given a penny to a beggar?"

"Ah," said Janey.

This was not quite kind nor yet quite fair, since Topsy gave generously of his time and from his pocket, though he was more interested in curing the cause of poverty than in the momentary alleviation of its results. It may be Janey only played that not unusual game of loving wives: to denigrate the husband. But Gabriel was encouraged. Perhaps, as Browning had said of quite a different sort of person, he had a heart too soon made glad.

And Janey, if you were one of those who admired her, did look very beautiful that day. In their new home in Queen Square, Bloomsbury, which like the Red House was filled with colours that glowed like dark jewels, she was stretched upon a great couch, her long limbs clothed in peacock blue that followed the lines of her spare body with the weight of water. One long hand hung on her breast in an archaic gesture, from her tall neck as from a stem her pale face drooped, framed in the masses of her curiously crisped hair. Her downward gaze, that day, was contemplative: perhaps she had the toothache.

It seemed to Christina Rossetti that in many ways Jane Morris and Elizabeth Siddal resembled one another. "Two brides from the same year," she would recall, and perhaps think it perverse in her brother to be attached to both. Each was tall, thin, and ailing, and though one was crowned with gold and one with jet, each was a daughter of Faery. Whether they were beautiful, whether they were brilliant, whether they were remarkable women or mere oddities, none could agree.

A long time afterward, young men came from all over England to see the legendary Mrs. Morris. Upon one of these, the young vegetarian George Bernard Shaw, she pressed a second portion of pudding.

"That will do you good," she said. "There's suet in it."

He never again could see her as a sibyl.

On the other hand, the impressionable Swinburne chose to worship. "The idea of marrying her is insane," he said. "To kiss her feet is the utmost men should dream of doing."

In her presence, Gabriel was transformed. The guiltless mischief-maker returned — the happy, brilliant seducer of them all — disguised only by the fact that the soft curls sat higher on his brow and that a full mustache now camouflaged the full and sensuous mouth. And then he suddenly had an idea.

Among students of the genus there is sharp disagreement as to whether the artist's mind is singularly simple or singularly devious. Certain it is that to the execution of their art they admit no impediment; it seemed reasonable to Gabriel that since he had conceived of a painting that was to be his best (the new one is always to be the best), Janey's time, without regard to her children, her household, or her husband, should be his own.

When William Morris, dressed in his artisan's smock and corduroys, appeared in the doorway, Gabriel cried, "I must have her!"

Now Morris was rather of the same way of thinking. Like Ruskin, he believed that man's salvation lies only in the joy of honest labour; like Rossetti, he believed the creation of beauty to be the most honest of labours.

"See," Gabriel said, and pulling Janey to her feet he moulded her like a mannequin, bending the head to a downward turn, resting the hands upon the breast, and moving each long, square finger until it looked as if they closed on something.

"Now look up," he said, and Janey raised those heavy eyes.

Gabriel said, "My Persephone."

Topsy remembered how, like an elder brother, Gabriel had encouraged him, and he rejoiced to see the fire of enthusiasm once again in the haunted eyes.

Then too, his trust in his friend was very great.

"Splendid!" he said.

So Janey Morris, a sombre, gorgeous wraith with her head bowed beneath the weight of her piled hair, began to slip back and forth between Queen Square and 16 Cheyne Walk.

Inside, the furry little wombats dozed. Outside, in the great disordered garden, the peacocks shrieked in derision.

21

ALAS! Man is insatiable. Once there was a beloved in his life again, Gabriel's thoughts turned back to his lost poems. Fanny, serving the morning eggs (Meredith had once said they were like bloody eyes), found Gabriel hunched at the table and chewing at a thumb.

"Now what's up?" she asked.

"Nothing you'd understand."

"Try me, Rizzetty," she said.

Though whatever it was it might very well be something she didn't understand, or at least didn't hold with. Why, with his paintings selling now like hotcakes, did he bother about them poems? Great smashing ladies they were that Mrs. Morris sat for and that he gave funny names. *La Pia* was one, and *Reverie* — which Fanny thought wasn't spelled right — and one called *Aurea Catena*. He said it meant the golden chain, and there in the picture was the chain — but where was it now? Fanny liked to keep track of his valuables.

He even sold the big cartoons that he prepared before the paintings and spoke of getting an assistant, which she thought made sense. Maybe if he did the cartoons, the fellow could slap on the paint. She herself slapped the eggs down and sat heavily. Why, business was so brisk that he already had that Howell to help with letters — a dark, flashy cove and good company.

"Cheer up, Rizzetty," she said cheerfully. "I found the dormouse as was missing. Curled up in the teapot he was, cosy as could be, but it give your friend Mr. Dodgson quite a start."

"Hold your tongue," Gabriel said. And then because he was very fond of her: "I'm sorry, Fanny. Pay no attention."

Very well, she wouldn't.

What darkened his days again was the dread fact that the first fruits of his genius, the lyrics and ballads that he believed to have a truer magic than those of Tennyson or Browning or Swinburne or of Christina, were still in Lizzie's clutches.

His brother had told him not to do it. "It does you honour," he had said. "But it is needless."

"No." And Gabriel had shuddered. "They took me from her when she needed me. Now they shall go with her."

And so for that first time, wild with grief and guilt, he had entered the room where she lay and looked down on his wife.

They had told him she looked as though she were alive; so much so that the dear Old Brown had wanted to call upon other doctors and had not been easily persuaded. The thick colour had drained from her face and the convulsed features were clear and still; as he stood above her now he saw that even the little lines of care and petulance had been smoothed away by the great palm of death. She was very beautiful.

And so he lifted the long, springing, riotous golden hair and placed against her cheek the leather notebook that held all his poems. So be it.

But oh, his beauties underneath the ground! Jenny, and Helen of Troy, and Queen Blanchelys, and the other Helen.

(O Mother, Mary Mother,
Three days, three nights, between Hell and Heaven!)

And the Blessed Damozel herself, who should lean from the gold bar of heaven, still lay instead in the Highgate Cemetery with Lizzie Siddal.

The William Bell Scotts and Miss Alice Boyd, who was forty now and still pretty, had an arrangement which struck everyone as curious, and which suited them better than it did Miss Boyd's relatives. She lived with the Scotts through the winters, and through the summertimes they lived with her. To some this seemed peculiar and to some irregular, but then Miss Boyd was very rich, and, as Will Little knows, much is permitted to the very rich. Perhaps her relatives had some private reservations.

Penkill Castle lay in wild and romantic Ayreshire country and possessed everything that might appeal to the poetic soul: moats, courts, and battlements which frowned down upon glens, rushing torrents, glimpses of silver sea. And there were seventeenth-century additions and nine-teenth-century water closets too, so that guests were as comfortable as they were bewitched. Even Christina Rossetti visited there and gazed pensively from the deep casements — though one cannot be sure that it was the wild scenery that caused her to be pensive.

It was decided by his friends that Gabriel Rossetti should for a time be sequestered at Penkill, where he could be idle and take the air. However, Gabriel would not go.

It was the summer of 1869. All that had seemed so san-guine seemed so no longer. Janey was ill and William Morris had taken her abroad, to the spa at Bad Ems, to

take the cure. Without her Gabriel was irritable, overex-
citable, and overanxious, and William Michael suspected
that he drank himself into what sick sleep he got.

Everyone blamed someone else.

All were agreed that Fanny Cornforth was at fault, but
no one said so because her presence was not openly recognized. Holman Hunt blamed Swinburne and Swinburne
blamed Holman Hunt. It cannot be said that William Michael blamed Jane Morris. However, in his papers and his
correspondence, he never mentioned her by name again.

Fanny blamed Charles Augustus Howell, and though her
reasoning was wrong, her instinct was right.

Howell had first appeared among them as secretary to
the innocent Ruskin but had quarreled with him and had
gradually graduated to Gabriel, for whom he performed
little kindnesses. Gabriel, at times so lavish with his money,
was acting now as if another shilling would never cross his
palm.

"X has turned a bad lot," he complained in one letter.
"Just as he was beginning to buy, he has got engaged to
get married, and is done for."

But Howell so badgered X that he bought a painting for
his bride. And Howell turned up new purchasers and
hounded old ones and attended public sales in order to bid
the prices up and in short, proved invaluable.

He was half Portuguese, half honest, and wholly un-
scrupulous, and, like Disraeli and Gabriel Rossetti, had too
much glitter for an Englishman. But there was no malice
in those gentlemen; in Howell, there was malice. Where he
could gain, there he attached himself; it may be that he
liked to manipulate. At any rate, although Ruskin was
caustic and William Michael uneasy, he had become Gabriel's intimate and toady.

"I don't know why you bother with him," Fanny said.
"He keeps you all stirred up."

Teasing her, Gabriel said, "Why then, you've changed your tune."

Only because she thought that Howell was changing Gabriel's tune, and the new one did not sit sweetly in her ears. She thought that they were up to something; whatever it was, it had Gabriel nervous as a cat. She had almost got used to Mrs. Morris and her useless ways; Jane didn't even sew a seam while she sat around being decorative, but could be excused a lot because she didn't keep Gabriel from Fanny's bed of nights. When Howell was in the house, she didn't see Gabriel from nightfall to noon.

In early summer, he sat one night late with Howell. Outside, rain whipped the new leaves; within, through the big, dim rooms the shadows shifted in the leaping candle flames. The rain demanded at the windows, retreated, and returned to knock again; the monkeys slept and woke. Between the men the whiskey bottle moved back and forth.

"I cannot do it," Gabriel said. "I dare not. There are those who would destroy me."

"Everyone wants to destroy," Howell said. "Look around."

"But that's a pack of wolves out there."

"So?"

"I wouldn't have a buyer left."

"Why, they'd be sniffing and begging at your door. Wolves like a whiff of brimstone."

Gabriel tipped the bottle and the whiskey flowed sweet as the waters of Lethe. But careful as he was, his wrist jumped and his fingers trembled as he eased the bottle back.

"Observe that," he said bitterly. "And I'm a painter."

Howell said: "You are a poet, too. That's where the tin is."

At some time while they talked the storm had ceased; now, in the silence, a broken branch tapped at the glass.

"My God!" Gabriel cried. "What's that?"

In long steps Howell reached the window and threw it wide; the watery sky was lightening, the ground mist walked in the shrubbery, the air poured cold and fresh.

"Only another morning of another day." And Howell turned, grinning. "Get out of town," he counseled. "Leave it all to me."

Gabriel ran his fingers through his soft curls; his hot Italian eyes searched the amused face of his mentor.

"All right," he said. "I'll go."

"Whatever can be the matter with dear Mr. Rossetti?" asked Miss Losh.

Nothing the ladies had been able to do had suited. He was supposed to have rest, but hour after hour they could hear him pacing his bedchamber, which was above the room in which they drank their tea, and heard his golden voice, though distant as through water, as he declaimed what dear Scott said were fine new sonnets.

And he was supposed to keep regular hours but, alas, night after night the men sat late while the port remained untouched and in the whiskey decanter the level fell. At breakfast, Scott was up with quip and jest, but the poet remained in his room and came down haggard and unsociable.

It had been determined that he was to set aside all usual concerns, but he haunted the great hall waiting for the mail and like a man in fever searched first for letters from London and then from Germany, seized on the odd one that did arrive, and the next day he searched again, insatiable.

He was supposed to get the air and did, dragging poor Scott out in all weathers to tramp the glen and climb the low hills, desperate for fatigue. On those long walks, Scott said, his conversation was disordered and spasmodic and dealt at an unhealthy length with sin and retribution.

Only Miss Losh could bring a smile to the sardonic lips

and a light to the great dark eyes beneath their bar of black brow. Miss Losh, as wealthy as her cousin and as eccentric, took quite a fancy to the difficult guest, and, being totally unworldly, prided herself upon her knowledge of the world.

"Mr. Rossetti," she said one afternoon at tea, "may an old lady beg a moment of your time?"

When they were left alone she hemmed and hawed and then, having flushed up to the ribbons on her cap, she humbly asked if she could be of any use.

"For it is very foolish," she explained, "that I, who require nothing, should possess so much and have it idle, if a few pounds could relieve that anxiety that I believe often — and most unjustly — disturbs the glorious labour of the artist."

For the first time in many weeks Gabriel forcibly restrained his laughter.

He said only, but with gentle warmth, "My dear lady."

Her bright old eyes searched his face. "Oh, good!" she said. "You are not offended?"

So he allowed Miss Losh to extend to him a few pounds and later a few more, to the total of some five hundred — which was pleasant for them both, because while he was not in any immediate need, sooner or later he was bound to be; and she had a nice little secret and a vested interest in his well-being and success. She never pressed him for her pounds; nor, to her credit, was the debt discovered until long after she had died. And to Gabriel's credit, it must be said that all his life he spoke very kindly of her.

But money alone could not cure Gabriel, in whom two separate beings struggled: the genius and the gentleman — one mad for recognition and the other maddened by the remedy he sought.

The remedy was desperate indeed.

There came a dark afternoon when Alice Boyd walked

out with the men. William Bell Scott made a curious choice, considering the nervous irritability of his friend, for it was his suggestion that Gabriel had not yet seen one of Penkill's most majestic sights.

The Devil's Punchbowl was a deep, black whirlpool formed in a basin at the foot of a waterfall that plunged from the top of a steep ravine; above it, and safely back from the craggy edge of the chasm, the three stopped to gaze down. Overhead, grey clouds scudded by until the turmoil of the sky mirrored the waters below.

"Stand back a bit, do," Alice Boyd said.

But Gabriel looked long, down to where the circling water whirled, speeding fast and faster to the deep spinning centre of the pool. Did he, at the dark heart of that hypnotic motion, see something that the others did not see?

"There, that's enough," Alice said nervously.

Scott placed her gloved hand on his own arm and patted it. The ladies, bless them, are easily alarmed. But then he shouted and lunged forward, for he had seen the tremor of Gabriel's cloak, the thrust of his shoulders, and his first uncertain, wavering step toward that end.

"My God!" he condemned.

"No," Gabriel said. "I do not think I meant so."

And, "I really do not think so," he said, shaken and pallid as they retreated through the thickening dusk to where Penkill Castle stood shrouded among its tall, sombre trees.

"I think not," Gabriel said.

Had he resisted some infinitely appealing call to the sleep for which he battled every night? But they were not to know, because where the torturous footpath met the shaven lawns an odd thing happened — a modest thing, but inexplicable and strange.

Out of the gathering shadows at their feet a chaffinch fluttered, a brown little bird that flew to Gabriel and fastened upon his hand. For a moment he stood like one of

Thomas Woolner's marble men, and then he shuddered and tried to throw it off; the wings beat frantically but the claws clung. When his hand stilled, the bird did too and, nestling, began to preen its quieting feathers.

Gabriel's eyes were coals in an ashen face. Scott stepped and knocked the finch away. Then Gabriel spoke.

"Lizzie's come back," he said.

And later, when they sat cold and silent at their tea, at the great gate below the bell rang and rang. They looked at one another.

For there was no one there.

For days after Gabriel went back to London the others still heard him overhead, pacing and reading. Nobody knows how this could have happened, but it did — or so Scott always claimed, and to the end, Mrs. Scott supported him; but then, loving wives do that. By that time, Miss Losh was not there to witness. And then again, Scott himself was a poet of sorts.

But many wonder if what Rossetti saw looking up at him from the Devil's Punchbowl was the face of his wife:

Sleepless with cold, commemorative eyes . . .

For on an October evening in 1869, they raised Elizabeth Siddal's casket from its grave. Charles Augustus Howell and Dr. Lewellyn Williams of Kennington, their faces muffled in their greatcoats, stood listening to the muttered imprecations of the gravediggers and the rattle and clang of shovels. It was a still night with a heavy mist; on the bordering trees clear drops clung, and as the bonfires leaped, from moment to moment the dark trees dazzled with their own watery fire.

The great fires were against infection; Dr. Williams had nothing better to suggest.

It had not been easy to arrange. The assiduous Howell had pursued, from dingy office to dingy office, the proper authorities, only to have them glance at their colleagues with their eyebrows raised.

"But my good man. Impossible, you know, without the permission of the family."

"But the deceased was the legal wife of Dante Gabriel Rossetti."

Ah, yes.

"But the land where she lies is the legal possession of the family."

To ask from William Michael permission for a deed so bizarre? Of Maria and Christina, to disturb the dead? Of the mother, permission to desecrate the ground where her sainted husband lay?

Never.

Then Howell bethought him of the Home Secretary. Mr. Bruce was an acquaintance, if not a personal friend, and by applying to him his own impudence, effrontery, and persistence, Howell succeeded where a gentleman would have failed.

The casket opened, Howell stepped forward eagerly, but was restrained by the grip of his companion. Dr. Williams felt his responsibility and it happened that the lady had once consulted him, so that he was in a position to verify that this was, in fact, the body of Elizabeth Eleanor Siddal. What a faux pas if in their stealth and haste they had disinterred a stranger!

Accustomed as he was to surprises, Dr. Williams had to suppress an exclamation because the lady was so extraordinarily preserved, and he wondered if perhaps the quantities of the drug from which she died could have had anything to do with the circumstances; it would make an interesting paper. But now he beckoned soberly to Howell.

Even that individual was taken aback as he gazed down to where the scarlet firelight mingled with the gold wealth that tumbled about the shoulders of Rossetti's wife. This, then, was the strange beauty whose painted image had changed the taste of England?

Howell had not thought to hesitate but did so while the diggers waited, their honest British faces cruelly metamorphosed by the leaping shade and light. He was an inquisitive man, but even his curiosity had been satisfied, and now there remained the price he had agreed to pay for that satisfaction. With a gloved hand he leaned and withdrew the peculiar treasure.

With the damp volume there came away a long lock of the thick golden hair.

22

"THERE IS a great hole," Gabriel complained, "right through the middle of *Jenny*."

Each page of the saturated manuscript had blurred and dimmed and the buckled cover was mossy to the touch. Nevertheless, and just as he had hoped, many of the lost lines came back to him or could be dredged from the memory of his friends; furthermore, the sight of his own words kindled new fires. He turned savagely on Howell. But of what Howell had returned to him, he wrote:

> Even so much life hath the poor tress of hair
>   Which, stored apart, is all love hath to show
>   For heart-beats and for fire-heats long ago . . .

Critics of Dante Gabriel Rossetti may complain of the tidbit that he then flung the British public, though it may be that his hope for the tenacity of the soul was as great as his fear.

Even so much life endures unknown, even where,
    'Mid change the changeless night environeth,
    Lies all that golden hair undimmed in death.

Then with the cautious husbandry of the artist Gabriel
saw that every line he wrote to Jane could be read as a
commemoration of his wife. Why, even Willowwood!

"Oh ye, all ye that walk in Willowwood,
    That walk with hollow faces burning white;
What fathom-depth of soul-struck widowhood,
    What long, what longer hours, one lifelong night . . ."

Would that not persuade them? Though he had written of
his fear of losing Jane.

Better all life forget her than this thing,
    That Willowwood should hold her wandering!

And in the future he would change every mention of
Janey's jetty hair to yellow.

But Lizzie had never liked to share.

"How is your interesting friend?" asked Mrs. Little.

"Not well. Not well at all, I fear."

"Fear or hear?" asked his mother.

This was not nice, because she knew that Will was
sentimental about his friends and both proud and chagrined
at how they had succeeded. And he remained on speaking
terms with them; his card was always welcome. But he
did not take it unkindly; his mother liked to quiz him a
bit as, to be sure, he did her. They had become companion-
able.

Now he looked at her with approval. For an old lady —
heavens! he approached forty and she must be all of fifty-
six — she was quite pretty and most soignée. Fond as she
was of simplicity in others, for herself she liked a little

grandeur, and her morning dress, though fresh as a spring flower, had a little train. She said it kept her ankles warm.

And then, he liked his mother's drawing room; here was ease! Tender hues, rose-shaded lamps, reposeful couches with silken downy cushions, velvets and sweet-scented flowers; in one corner a china Cupid large as a two-year-old proffered china roses.

"Ah," Will said. "You have a new desk?" His brows rose. A writing desk in the drawing room? And yet it was a pretty thing, made of marquetry, inlaid with lemonwood and as graceful as it could manage with its little bow legs.

"About the desk," she said, and her fine eyes dropped. "I have a little secret, Will." He would understand why she would not wish it known. "I am about to be an authoress."

And then she hastened to add, "Oh, not a scandal like George Eliot, Will. But everyone is doing it, you know, and though I am not like to prove a Ouida, we do have our little plans."

Pray, whom was he to understand by "we"?

Oh, a few of her friends. Letitia Tiverton and Lady Quarles. Having observed that the ties of polite society were loosening, they purposed a sort of guide to assist better young women against vulgarities. Who should know better than Lady Quarles?

"It will be called only *The Gentlewoman's Guide* and will be published by subscription, so there will be no cost to us, you see. Will you want tea?"

Will straightened his checked trousers so that the braid ran straight from hip to the outer ankle. His pointed pumps shone.

"And who will write which part?" he asked.

Her answer was evasive. "Oh, what we know best, you see. What to wear abroad and where to seat clergymen."

"And what, Mama, do you know best?" Although he knew full well.

"Well, dear," she said. She touched the heavy coil of hair that topped her head and brushed the feathery curls before her ears. "*Well*, dear. Of course my friends know of your interests, and so I shall take the arts."

"Demme!" said Will.

"Now Will," she said reasonably, "they're everywhere these days. I understand John Millais is received by the Queen. And Will, since the Burne-Joneses bought The Grange and the Ford Madox Browns have that great barracks in Fitzroy Square, one must be so careful. A young friend of mine saw that strange Mrs. Morris dressed in loose ivory velvet and sitting on a sort of throne, and Will, Mr. Rossetti *crouched* at her feet and fed her strawberries from a spoon. Now Will, you know we can't have that."

Will was on his feet in a trice. On the pretty desk, with the pen tray and sealing wax and inkstand, there was a book of blank pages bound in soft white leather. He opened it and read her spidery writing.

> . . . the widow who considers with seriousness whether she will best express her loss by a bonnet or a bow is already half consoled, and will ere long bestring herself with jet beads.

Well, that was inoffensive, though it had little to do with art.

"What you are looking for," his mother said, "comes later. You are so impatient, Will."

> What the lily-worshippers lack is a sense of form. Their model for a dress seems a sack, tied around the waist with a string, with two smaller sacks for sleeves; their hats are modelled on cabbage leaves and their indefinite curvatures very trying to all with any true feeling for architecture.

Of course she had a right to her opinion. Will thought about how the young girls this year had little middles and were swathed below with folds of silk that tucked up over their derrieres, slick and round as bubbles, and he thought his mother was right, but then, horrified, he read something she had no right to say.

A glance at the *Beata Beatrix* of Rossetti in the National Gallery is sufficient. Was it not enough to have her pallor rendered sickly by the red (as of the homely carrot) of her hair, that the artist deemed it necessary to array her so gruesomely in a green that suggests green-sickness, Robespierre, and the fading year?

"You can't say that," he said.

"Why not?" Why, he impugned her taste!

"Because," he said. "Because that was his wife."

She was a nice woman, though fluffle-headed. "Oh then, I wouldn't say it for the world." Though she spoke wistfully, because she did think it had been well put, and like all authors was pained to part with her words.

"You are still fond of him?" she asked.

Well, *fond* . . .

But yes, Will missed Gabriel's wild company, after which the tenor of his own reasonable days seemed to lack salt. With many another sober citizen at the zoo, he was fascinated by the preening and plumage of the exotic birds.

"I miss him, yes."

And to his own surprise he expatiated upon the woes by which the genius of his friend was threatened, including the cruel fortune of his wife, his failing sight, and, above all, the savage attacks of his insomnia.

His mother, who was perhaps not quite so sheltered as

he thought, listened, and her little beringed hands fluttered in distress.

"You can do nothing about most of that," she said, "but Will, there is no cause for him to go without his sleep!"

Whatever could she mean?

Why, there was lately a wonderful remedy; some German had discovered, and not long ago, a blessed substance of which twenty grains brought hours of safe and healthy sleep from which her friends — well, certain of her friends — habitually awoke clear-eyed and revivified. So clever at these things, the Germans.

Why, chloral hydrate!

And delighted to for once surpass her son's worldly wisdom, she cried gaily: "Nonsense! It wouldn't hurt a fly!"

23

WHAT WILL LITTLE reported happily to Gabriel
was that chloral hydrate had been offered to the
world in 1832 by an Herr Doktor J. von Liebig, who
claimed in it a powerful and safe hypnotic which produced no preliminary excitement and induced deep and
wholesome slumber.

He did not tell Gabriel that chloral hydrate, when mixed
with alcohol and ether, was a syrupy liquid with a greasy,
bitter taste and a pungent odor irritating to the eyes, and
that like many beneficent substances it was dangerous:
with misuse the patient became overexcited, loquacious,
easily fatigued, and habituated. Some had been known to
hallucinate.

How could Will Little tell Gabriel that? He didn't know.

But an American friend of William Michael's who had
been recently American consul in Crete did try to warn
him. The friend, William James Stillman, had recently
lost a young wife.

"This chloral," he said, "gives only a deathlike stupefaction without restorative power, and a suicidal despondency which I know too well."

Will had procured for Gabriel enough for three measured doses. Gabriel forgot about it for two nights and on the third, being by nature given to excess, he took it all. He slept far into the next day and having wakened inert and of heavy spirits, he put the thought of it away.

He didn't need it, anyway. For once, Dante Gabriel was happy.

All his life everyone — almost everyone — had loved Gabriel: men, women, and animals; and children surely would have loved him too had the circumstances of his life brought him into more contact with the little ones. Certainly quiet little Jenny Morris and her mercurial sister May were fond of him, or said they were. It may be that those who are too much beloved see enemies in those who may be but indifferent; Gabriel had been much cosseted by his friends. In March an old friend offered to Gabriel the rest and respite of her country house.

Madame Bodichon was that very Barbara Leigh-Smith who with robust good humour had hauled up her skirts and waded brooks and had arranged for Lizzie's convalescence at Hastings; and at Scalands there was a window upon which the three friends had scratched their initials. But poignant though that was, it did not threaten Gabriel's pleasure as he readied his poems for publishing. Nothing could have spoiled his joy, for in the very town where Lizzie had taken the sea air, Janey Morris, back at last from Ems, was now established. Gabriel could see her daily and alone, since Topsy Morris was too restless for any further rest cure and was soon back in London.

Some might think it insensitive of this pair to wander hand in hand where Lizzie had walked alone, and in the

very town where Gabriel had been a reluctant bridegroom
and she a wasted bride. But artists are insensitive. And perhaps Madame Bodichon should not have offered Scalands
at the same time to the other widower — for William
Stillman was also there, though briefly, and departed less
charmed by Gabriel than he had been at first. He could
put up with Gabriel's cavalier arrangement of space, hours,
and meals, but was annoyed when Gabriel would not pay
his share — not because he was penniless, but because he
preferred to purchase porcelain.

Or perhaps Gabriel acted with malice and forethought,
for as soon as Stillman had moved out, Jane Morris moved
in.

That sort of thing gives painters a bad name. Even
among their friends, what William Morris and Gabriel
Rossetti did next was incomprehensible: they assumed
the joint occupancy of a country house of their own, and
when Morris had established there his wife, his children,
and the companion of his youth, he departed within days
for Iceland.

Oddly enough, the gentle Georgiana Jones was most
offended by the news.

"My dear," said Ned, "I can most categorically assert
that Janey would do nothing wrong."

"Indeed, I hope that you are right," said Georgiana.

And her eyes fell to an annoying, rebellious knot in
her thread which positively demanded to be snapped by
her teeth, and was so disposed of. But she had put behind
an early and romantic admiration for Janey Morris; here-
after, the warmth of Georgiana's affection for Topsy
doubled, while that for his wife was halved.

There was an arguable reason for the Iceland trip.
Topsy was deep in the Nordic sagas and writing one of his
own.

Of *The Story of Sigurd the Volsung* Gabriel said: "I

never cared very much for all that stuff. How can one take a real interest in a man who has a dragon for a brother?"

Nonetheless, he was delighted by Topsy's departure, although the move caused great confusion at Cheyne Walk.

"Do you know what it costs," Fanny demanded, "to feed those hanimals? What do you want two houses for? It's one thing if a softheaded woman offers you a place, all found, but I'll be bound Mr. Topsy will want your share. You an't the most free with your money. Not with me, you an't."

Gabriel was stuffing into a portmanteau what had not gone into his big wicker trunk.

"Lumpses, I never starved you yet."

Fanny stood with her arms akimbo and her still lovely hair loose on her shoulders, and she sniffed.

"There's others like my company if you don't. I might have Mr. Schott come to call. Hughes don't appreciate it when he hangs around to home."

This Mr. Schott was a roomer at the Hugheses', and that was not the first time that Fanny had attempted to spur Gabriel's attention by the mention of the gentleman. But he said only: "By all means, Fanny. Keep him out of the wine cellar, though — there's a good Elephant."

Fanny tossed the hair that was yellow as daffodils. "And as for that," she said, "I might like a bit of a holiday myself. I might just show up at this here Kelmscott Manor."

Gabriel straightened from his task and glared at her; his voice was hard as cold steel.

"You will not even jest about that, Fanny; or you will leave this house forever and we shall no more be friends."

"I was just ragging you," she sulked.

"See that you were," he said.

Kelmscott Manor was old enough and odd enough to suit them all. Its deep stone walls were to prove cold in winter, and the arrangement of its many rooms more intriguing than convenient. In order to reach the chamber where he chose to work, Gabriel must pass through his bedroom. This had advantages. But there was no advantage in having to pass through the bedroom of the Morrises in order to reach the room in which they all chose to spend their evenings. Certainly it was no occasion for surprise to come across anyone, anywhere.

The gardens were walled, and beyond a profusion of yew hedges the land spread gently to the quiet waters of the Thames; it was on the riverbank on a high summer day that Gabriel, who had been playing with the little girls and then, impatient, had sent them away, lay with his head in Janey's lap.

Behold a happy man!

He has his fair lady but not her upkeep, and the pleasure of her children without responsibility for their futures. Almost overnight the publication of *Poems by D. G. Rossetti* (price twelve shillings) has made him a name to be reckoned with. To be sure, he took no chances but enlisted his friends as critics, and Swinburne and Morris — the one with his usual fire and the other a bit more uncertainly — have hailed in print the new Michelangelo. And to their praises were added those of doctor and don, barrister and both the lord and his lady. Tennyson had been cool and Browning silent, but the *Poems* had already cleared three hundred pounds.

Two things had disappointed Gabriel. The lively American market he had counted on had not materialized; Ralph Waldo Emerson had written to William Bell Scott, ". . . it does not come home to us, it is exotic; but we like Christina's religious pieces."

And then, the Franco-German War had broken out. "I suppose all poetry will be dead as ditch-water now," Gabriel said gloomily. How could Calliope compete with the Siege of Paris?

Nevertheless, he had been acclaimed the master of two arts.

"The only one since Blake," he said, awed.

"Topsy paints too," Janey told him.

"He does not. He decorates; it's not the same at all."

If Janey didn't agree, she didn't say so. Janey was restful because she said so little. She was the only woman he had known who could sit for hours with her hands idle.

The water meadows were alive with insects that hummed and sang and flashed infinitesimal wings in the sun; upon the river the light slid in golden sheets. Gabriel slept of nights. Because he now painted only in the north morning light his eyes did not hurt; he had been promised nine hundred pounds for a mere copy of *Beata Beatrix*, and the old poems which had so brutally obsessed him had given way to a new flood of song.

The desecration of Lizzie's grave had proved so much easier than he had thought. His brother — he had at last told William Michael — had blanched. "You have suffered long enough," he said. "But do not tell Mama."

It would not have occurred to Gabriel to tell his mother.

So he was free of that, or would be free if it were not for Howell, who like Mephistopheles presumed upon his silent knowledge. Janey had embroidered from Gabriel's own design a long curtain, against drafts, that was to hang between her bed and her husband's.

Howell said that it proved too short to keep her husband out at night.

Gabriel had slammed his hand on the table and said with an oath: "No! He would not dare!" And so had soiled his leman with a jakehouse joke. But that one sonnet in which he could not restrain his triumph he had respectably retitled *Nuptial Sleep*.

Tennyson, someone said, had called it filthy. But no one could know it was not written to Rossetti's wife.

Meantime, nothing had happened. No cold wind blew

through his room at night and no voice spoke his name. What had he feared? That Lizzie would be vengeful? Yes.

Now Janey said placidly, "I must go."

"Why, love?"

"Because the mail will have come."

There had been no word yet from Iceland for Topsy's wife.

Gabriel turned and swung over her and pressed her shoulders to the ground.

"I am making a song for you," he said. "Shall I tell it you, love?"

"And then I must go."

But she lay quietly while, each elbow upon the fan of her rough, dark hair, he spoke:

> On this sweet bank your head thrice sweet and dear
>   I lay, and spread your hair on either side,
>   And see the newborn woodflowers bashful-eyed
> Look through the rippling tresses here and there.

"But Gabriel," she said gravely, "the woodflowers are all blown."

Why should such a simple statement fill him with such unease? As if there rose from a damp ground the faint chill exhalation of dying winter that accompanies false spring, that debatable time between true seasons.

She stirred beneath him.

Debatable was a good word; yes, he would use it.

> On these debatable borders of the year
>   Spring's foot half falters . . .

"Swear that you love me, love," he said.

Those great, grave, empty eyes looked up, fringed with heavy lashes.

"Dearest Gabriel," she said.

So he released her. And he watched her regal figure as she paced, the dark head bent contemplatively, toward the summer blossoms spilled: cornflowers, larkspur, maiden's house, while from the shallow basket on her arm the rue.

III

Fanny

24

During the months when Gabriel was away Fanny sulked and had Mr. Schott over quite a lot, to the displeasure of Cook and the young man in a striped apron who fed the larger animals, answered the door, and threw fuel on the fires of Cook's indignation by telling of the laughter he heard late at night.

Gabriel wouldn't have minded. Fanny contributed vastly to his comfort and so, just as if she had been his wife, he wanted her there when he wanted to find her there, and about that he could depend on her.

The servants minded because he had never defined her position in the household. She didn't cook anymore but then, neither did Cook; it made more sense that everyone should rummage for himself. She was no member of the family, yet she was entrusted with the keys and, presumably, with the authority that went with them.

But for what? Could she dismiss the others if she chose? No one knew. Nor was Fanny anxious to find out, since the others helped to clear, if not to clean, the big old house;

and if they obstinately refused her their company she still knew that they were there — that was a dark old place.

"Not that I have to be alone," she said to an imaginary visitor. "If you take my meaning."

Taken and approved! If a woman won't stand up for her rights, who will?

That morning, Fanny imagined that she wore a gown of a light plum colour — no, maybe more of a powder blue, very nice with the masses of her blonde hair. She stretched her plump, pretty hand to the bellpull and her diamond blistered the air with light.

"What a pretty ring," said this visitor. "Open'anded, isn't he."

"When it suits."

But men were all like that; when it suited. Fanny's guest glanced appreciatively on the brass and ormolu, the tall vases filled with peacock feathers, the priceless blue porcelain.

"There's many a girl started out with more," the visitor admitted, "and ended up with less."

"Try to keep it all washed!" cried Fanny. "Try to keep it dusted!"

Not that she bothered — why should she? It was hard enough to keep your own person clean with the boy so grudging with the hot-water cans and a day's job to get the soap out of your hair. And then this woman who was supposed to be the best friend Fanny ever had said something sly.

She said, "Of course, tomorrow you could be back on the street."

Depends, don't it, on what you mean by that?

She never had been on the street, not Fanny, and any pound she earned she earned proper. A married woman she'd been too, all her grown life.

Fanny's laughter bubbled in her white, full throat.

When Gabriel came back there would be better games to
play. She stood, and feeling the hot blood course through
her eager body she kicked high, so that the heavy skirt fell
from the plump calf of her leg.

She always had thought that that there Mrs. Morris
was going to let him down.

Meantime, it was time to feed the chicking.

Summer, that sinister season, had fled with her dusty
skirts and fading garlands; her bawdy laughter echoed
no more through the sunny gardens. One chill rain and
another one brought down the last flags of the flowers and
plastered the leaves of the tall elms to the garden paths.
Autumn claimed the sweet banks where the lovers had lain
and sent his cold scouts to twitch the damp tapestries upon
the walls of Kelmscott Manor. On a wet, grey morning
when the weak fires surrendered meekly to the deep stone
walls of the old house, Jane Morris went back to London.
She said the children's health was delicate, which it was
not, and that the dark, cold house was dull for them,
which it was; and mindful of her own unsubstantial physical resources, she said she hoped to avoid another winter at
Ems.

"There will be other summers," she said kindly.

And of course she was right: the seasons come back;
it is the seasoners who do not return.

Janey was surely honest in what she pleaded, but it
may also be that the ardours of an impassioned poet,
though irresistible in the climate of a stolen hour, do not
hold the same appeal to a woman of domestic tendencies
when the man is under her own roof. Then she must be
aware of his breakfast eggs, the state of his dressing gown
and his medicines, and though it is nice to be hailed as the
angel of his life, it is perhaps not quite so nice, when he is
searching for a book, to be discovered in one's nightcap.

Whatever her reasons were, they did not include any fear of her husband. William Morris, that remarkable man, stood by his avowed principles: love cannot be commandeered nor loyalty compelled, and two names on a paper do not make a marriage.

If he suffered (and he did suffer), he was never less than gentle and kind to Janey nor less than courteous to his old friend, although between them there was never glad, confident morning again. This may have been a weakness in the man but some thought not, and there were those among their mutual friends who would have named him the manlier of the two.

So Gabriel was all alone that autumn of 1870 when there appeared among the ranks of the ghosts, phantoms, and warlocks which haunted his fevered fancy a concrete, veritable, determined, and powerful enemy — in the person of Robert Buchanan, who was determined to bring Gabriel Rossetti down.

He struck through *The Contemporary Review*, by means of an article called "The Fleshly School of Poetry," in which he accused Gabriel of prurience and vulgarity and named those sonnets called *The House of Life* a brothel and the poet's inamorata a harlot. If London was a moral cesspool, he suggested, the British public could thank Dante Gabriel Rossetti.

Ironically, his quarrel was not with Gabriel but with William Michael, who had described him as a pretentious poetaster, and with Swinburne, who had some time before aborted Buchanan's plans to edit Keats's poems. Buchanan was not a wicked man — only a small one.

He could not know that from his attack, Gabriel would take his heart's wound.

"I don't see what's so bad about it," Fanny said.

But then, she had read it as the "flashy" school of poetry and took it rather as a compliment.

Fanny was glad that she had filled the dim reaches
of the drawing room with flowers and that a fire burned
almost as if she'd known that he was coming (though the
chrysanthemums were in fact massed in and about the
blue china to disguise from William Michael that a piece
or two of value was missing). She was glad that she was
wearing her beet-coloured merino, too; Cook said she was
too stout for it, but it brought brass to her hair and cin-
namon to her cheeks and made her a woman a cold man
could warm his hands at.

"Go on," Gabriel said. "Go on — read the rest."

He had flung himself into a chair beside the fire; his
damp coat smelled of wool and his boots smudged the
fender, so it was just as well no one had bothered to polish
it. She bent her head over the offending journal.

"Coo!" she said after a moment. " 'e does think you write
dirty!"

Gabriel said, "I am a ruined man."

"Did you ever do this bloke an 'arm?" asked Fanny.
For though the critic's words were highfalutin, she recognized the instinct of the guttersnipe.

"I don't know," he said. "But I think that I have done
much harm."

His voice was amazed. Why, if you start thinking about
that, who is safe? And it is hard to determine who is
more dangerous — those like Fanny, who plan a good
deal of damage but never act on it, or those like Gabriel,
who damage without thinking and cannot make amends.

Gabriel thought on this and his shoulders in his greatcoat humped; his face was soiled with fear. He was both
superstitious and a Christian: Buchanan could ruin him
because he had earned ruin.

And Fanny looked at him with pity, remembering the
gallant youth whose gaze had long ago blazed at her and
who would have once rushed eagerly to battle. He was

not, she thought, the sort who should turn forty: he didn't know how to go about getting older.

So she went to him and held his hot face to her beet-coloured bosom.

"Ah, love," she said. "Come take a bit of comfort."

25

WHEN FANNY TURNED, she saw a big, blurred moon.

It swung on the horizon like a child's balloon, tied by a string of vapour, and its misty light washed through the open window and rinsed the bed in silver.

"Ah, look, Rizzetty," she said. "Look at the big moon."

He didn't answer and she thought he was funning her, but when she touched him he was stiff as sticks, so probably what she had done was wrong; she had just wanted to let in some air. She struggled out of the big bed, slammed the window down, and pulled the heavy draperies across; then he sighed and moved.

"Well, if you didn't like it then," she said crossly, "whyn'cha get up yourself?"

He said, "I don't know who's there."

How could anyone be there — *up* there?

She said, "You're joking."

He fumbled on the spindle-legged night table for his

glass, and she smelled the sour sharpness of the sleeping draught.

"You're joking?"

After a moment he said lightly, "Well, of course I'm joking."

But the more she thought about it, the more she wasn't sure. How do you know if a man is playacting? Particular, as she said to Hughes, if he drinks and takes that stuff? And then he wouldn't see his friends anymore but hid in his studio and refused them.

Hughes said, "You had ought to tell his brother."

But as the dark hours of that winter dragged into spring, William Michael, though he was troubled, preferred to think that Gabriel was out of sorts; and when he found him tight as a spring with excitement or foulmouthed with rage, he chose to consider only that his own visit was ill-timed. Of course he blamed Buchanan, but mildly censured Gabriel, too.

"He is bad-tempered," he said. "He still licks his wounds."

Frances Lavinia, as strong-minded mothers do, had withdrawn from her children now that they were grown. She sat with her folded hands on her black lap, heavier now than she had been but still as beautiful, with her fine mouth and brilliant eyes; from her iron hair the soft ties of her widow's cap depended.

She said, "It was always the dearest wish of my heart that my children should be intellectual, but I had hoped they would have common sense."

This was a little thrust at William Michael, so inordinately attached to little Lucy Brown, who was not altogether agreeable. Since he had stayed comfortably a bachelor so long, she saw no need now for him to undertake a domestic establishment.

But she did not exclude the others. Maria's religious

zeal she thought excessive and Christina, though they lived in the same house, she seldom saw. Perhaps the dear girl confused asceticism with personal pride; she had become morbidly shy as physical disorders robbed her of her wood-thrush beauty, thickening her fragile body and pushing forth the extraordinary eyes.

And Gabriel, who had been his father's favourite, saw enemies everywhere and was inattentive to his mother.

"Your brother is very like his dear Papa," she said. "But at the bottom, is a person of good sense."

But Fanny knew that when he closed himself into his studio he did not paint, and that when he hunched above his desk it was to scribble appeals to those whom he still thought his friends praying they defend him; many of these letters he destroyed as he struck name after name from the roster of the trusted and added each to the lengthening list of conspirators. Those few he sent were often marked *Burn This*.

For Gabriel knew they were tampering with his mail.

"No, Rizzetty!" Fanny said, shocked. "I wouldn't let nobody touch your letters!"

To Brown, who had been much kept from him by the gout, he urged the use of sealing wax and a sixpenny seal. "There have been some very equivocal postage incidents lately," he wrote darkly. "Another desirable point is to use envelopes thick enough to prevent letters from being read *through* them."

"I'd never!" Fanny told him hotly.

But Gabriel did not mean the dear old Elephant. He meant that public servants were being bribed. "I enclose you the envelope of your letter," he continued. "The *bottom* of it looks very queer."

Only Fanny knew how much he drank to ease the blinding pain that struck now at his forehead and now at his nape, or that while he boasted to his brother of diminished dosages of chloral, he was running up a hidden bill with a second apothecary, or that when he came to her bed he wanted only to have his trembling body held through the sleepless nights.

Only Fanny knew he kept a full bottle of laudanum in his room.

Will Little at forty looked like a child disguised — rather a natty child. On a June day he observed, with satisfaction, his image in the glass. His suit was of the newest cut and suitable for a morning call; at the high closing the jacket buttoned once and then hung open to display the spotless vest; the sleeves were cuffed and the trousers narrowed to his pumps. With this he wore a small, rounded hat with a curled, narrow brim much like the one he had worn some years before except that that had been adorned with a soft little tie that floated down behind.

His mother had giggled when she saw it. Never mind.

He had a need today to be at his best because he was about to succour an old friend who did not want his succour. But Gabriel had gone too far, and Will was not so shallow that he would not risk a snub in order to help him.

An elementary caution was the small coin that Gabriel would not tender Caesar. His warfare with Buchanan was the scandal of the year and the very ladies at the tea table were twittering. Ever since those strange Brontë women the ladies had shown exorbitant interest in dark, rebellious gentlemen of a sort whom they would not have admitted to their drawing rooms and from whom they would have hustled their daughters in all haste. But their own encounters with such gentlemen were only through Mudie's circulating library, at small cost to themselves, while it is men who purchase paintings. Now men are not drawn much to rebellious males, particularly when the rebellion takes the form of not producing the picture which the purchaser has purchased, and they are likely to confuse this habit with the habit of keeping loose women in the house and armadillos in the garden.

"Though some have said," Will's mother had reported, "that it is not at all a menagerie he keeps, but a harem."

What a canard! "Who says such a thing?"

"Why, Lady Tiverton, for one. And it is true, is it not, that from time to time he and Mrs. Morris have lived together?"

"They share a domicile," Will had said stiffly.

"Well, there!" his mother said merrily.

Along Cheyne Walk landlords now wrote into the lease that tenants should not harbour peacocks, and on one occasion the armadillo had burrowed through the floor of a neighbour's kitchen and caused the cook hysterics.

And Will was not the only one who objected. The faithful Brown himself had protested, "You cannot continue this ridiculous way of life!"

"Whatever do you mean?" Gabriel had said, blandly.

So it was up to Will to make him see that people were speaking very dangerously of him, and he thought that he would begin with that friend of his mother's who had called Gabriel "mysterious and macabre."

"And one cannot forget," that friend had said, "that there has always been some question about his tragic past."

Will was truly sorry to bring up the ambiguity surrounding Lizzie's death, but if there were still those who questioned the possibility of Gabriel's complicity, then he must not be allowed to forget.

Nor could he be permitted to overlook the extent to which the character of his own work contributed to his unsavoury reputation. For Buchanan had started up an avalanche. *The Quarterly Review* had just decried the "animal passions" depicted in the *Poems* and had termed the sonnets "emasculated obscenity."

But even worse than what was said in print was what

was said in whispers. The American novelist Henry James called Gabriel "more or less sinister," and the English-man Samuel Butler named him "horrid" and said that he was "wrapped up in self-conceit and lives upon adulation." Most pusillanimous was Robert Buchanan himself, who had defended his article on the score that it would "do good to the men criticized, perhaps even saving them from go-ing headlong to Hell."

Was that not impudent? Will thought. It might well be that Gabriel should call him out!

The most unkindest cut had come from Robert Brown-ing. Browning was not in the best of tempers, having (not long enough after the death of his wife) proposed to Louisa, Lady Ashburton, who refused him. But that did not excuse him from accepting a gift copy of the *Poems* and then saying of it that it was "accented with poetry, as it were — like trifles of various sorts you take out of a cedar or a sandalwood box." And then of ending in a temper, "I hate the effeminacy of his school!"

That would indeed be a blow to Gabriel, but he must not be allowed to put his confidence where it was not warranted.

So absorbed had Will been in his own thoughts that he was almost surprised to find himself already before the low wall that separated 16 Cheyne Walk, Chelsea, from the cobbled road upon which, now, his cabman rattled away. Over the bow windows that bulged for two stories upward, ivy clawed raggedly at the mortisework. Far above, a naked life-sized statue pointed to the sky with one leg high in a posture of potential flight. Why, it was an immense house, a preposterous house; he knew that fire insurance alone cost Gabriel eight hundred pounds — al-though in Will's opinion the place was more likely to topple than to burn.

And suddenly he was hesitant. It is all very well to speak of the satisfaction of having done one's duty, but he hadn't done it yet, and Gabriel, upon occasion, could turn quite fierce. Then he bethought him of something that was bound to help.

Gabriel had never been much interested in wars, but during the Siege of Paris, Camille Pissarro and Claude Monet had both been in England — whether to escape the antagonism of the Salon or to avoid eating rats, Will did not know. But he had met them. Why, even as the Pre-Raphaelites so long ago, these men now battled for the destruction of all that had gone before them!

True that these new brooms — some were so unkind as to say their canvases appeared to be painted with their brooms — rejected all that the PRB had battled to establish, but Gabriel's generous heart would surely rejoice with all who revolt, and these new men, along with Sisley, Renoir, Manet, and Cézanne, were in one way going to imitate the PRB: were they refused once more by the Salon, they planned in 1874 to exhibit by themselves and would, as certainly as those who had gone before, prevail.

Now there was a secret bound to distract and cheer!

And feeling himself ever so much more cheerful, Will tucked his walking stick beneath his arm, reached for the great brass tarnished knocker, and briskly knocked.

Noon is an ugly time of day. Even here in the bowels of the old house a bald and hot sun, dirty with dust motes, pried past the heavy curtains and lanced Gabriel's eyes with light. The morning's promise had died with the dew; the little leaves curled on the trees and hung motionless, the shadow of each inert as a lead coin. Cool evening with kind veils was weary hours away. Fanny Cornforth opened the door and found Gabriel alone and motionless.

"Oh, there you are," she said.

Fanny was dressed for the street; a small hat rode the masses of her hair at an unlikely angle, she carried a parasol beribboned with blue and heavy with roses as the

June day itself, and the yards of material that covered
her stomach and were swept back in folds and bunches at
her rear did little for her sturdy shape, and failed to amuse
Gabriel.

"Your friend's gone already, then?"

He said, "It appears that I have no friends."

"Well, I like that!" she said.

Since the abrupt departure of his visitor, Gabriel had
been brooding about new enemies and old friends. Where
were they, whose doors and purses never had been closed
to him?

"Ah," Fanny said. "They're all married men. They can't
traipse around the way they used to do."

Gabriel alone had no wife, no child, and no home, except this ancient labyrinth that housed ghosts. Now they
conspired to take his name from him, which was his only
defense to posterity.

A clear voice spoke a loud obscenity.

Someone unauthorized, uninvited, and unwelcome was
in his house. He looked quickly at Fanny, who must be
pretending not to hear; she was buttoning her gloves. Not
content now to spread evil about him and to blacken his
name with questions he could not answer and charges that
would rob him of the little he had achieved (for they were
right, he was no Michelangelo), they would now invade
his privacy and like Sicilians, press their vendetta even
to his person, would they?

But who? Whose contempt for him could be so great
unless they understood him? Perhaps the handful to whom
in perplexity he had turned for technical advice. That
could be Holman Hunt, who had called Fanny "that large-
throated, disagreeable woman" and had said of him (oh,
he had heard; somebody always takes it upon himself to
be sure that you hear) that he no longer painted anything
but "women of voluptuous nature."

Or Millais, who had grown so grand. Or like Iago, snarling behind the mask of friendship, Brown. Brown?

No — *Browning!*

He saw it clearly now, by the foul glare that Will had lit: it was all true. There was conspiracy — vast, dire and dangerous — and Robert Browning was behind it; Buchanan was but his lackey and his tool. Why? Oh, a fool knew why. Because out of silence there had come a new singer to rob Browning of his lyre.

But it was not Browning who spoke now but Browning's hired unseen assassin — and with blasphemy. Gabriel whirled, livid-eyed.

"Who's in this house?"

Fanny said: "I don't know, I'm sure, without it's your brother. He's coming with that man."

William Michael was too trusting, too innocent. What man?

"Then let them show themselves," he said. "No, stop. I won't see them."

"But there's a cheque in it. Rizzetty, we need that cheque!"

"Then you must stay with me."

And now a strange thing happened, because as Gabriel spoke, what he said seemed to echo from some different place, some different time.

"Where are you going? You are not going out?"

"You know where I'm going," Fanny said, troubled. "Don't pertend you don't. I'm going to Hughes because I promised and he's sick."

"I implore you, do not leave me."

He knew that these words had been said before, that all had taken place before, that the conclusion already had occurred and that nothing now could be changed but spun instead toward an inevitable goal.

Fanny said — and somehow it seemed the worse because

her words were not ungentle — "But I got to go, I owe it to him. You owe him, too."

If she left, it would be all up with him. He knew this. He could not face alone the gathering dusk, the whispering voices, the malignant and implacable enemy. This time chloral could only weaken and dull his defenses; his fear was the more maniacal because he did not know what he feared unless it was the agony of fearing.

"Don't go," he said. "*I warn you.*"

Fanny straightened the little hat that rode like a boat on the billows of her light hair. She kissed him tenderly, she said he was her foolish child, she said she would be back tomorrow.

Then she smiled. The door closed behind her.

And Gabriel knew who had said all this before him.

Two things return to trouble those who survive: you saw nothing and you did nothing (oh, you saw nothing, did you not?). But everyone from time to time says something or does something that is unreasonable, and it is possible that you did not hear correctly or did not see what you thought you saw — therefore you erred. But you did not err. It was not convenient for you at that time to see; you thought, as William Michael thought, that a good night's sleep would do wonders.

When William Michael arrived with a customer, Gabriel turned his back on them both.

"You are under no obligation, sir," he said, "to take this painting, nor I to part with it; least of all to someone who scorns me as a poet and a man."

Mr. Lefevre managed to depart with his painting anyway and without his cheque. But William Michael lingered, frightened at last by Gabriel's excited and meandering speech. Gabriel had determined that Tennyson took no part in this assault upon his reason, but Ruskin was surely

and bitterly involved. Ruskin had been first to defect where
he had once befriended, and most sinister of all, he had
always taken Lizzie's part.

"For it is she, of course!" Gabriel cried. "It is she!"

At this point William Michael sent for Dr. Hake, and
that good man for a Dr. Maudsley, whom Gabriel denounced as an impostor.

"He is no physician!" he said hotly. "He is an emissary
of evil! Cannot you see?"

Dr. Maudsley clucked gently and recommended gruel
and bed rest. In these sad cases sleeplessness was usual
and should be relieved with paraldehyde. Spirits and drugs
should be gradually reduced and above all the patient
should not be left alone.

To their surprise, the patient consented, stipulating
only that he be allowed to retreat to Fanny's room, where
his enemies might not find him, and that first he be permitted to remove from his own bedchamber his nightgown,
his razor, and his leather-bound book of poems, lest on his
return he find it clawed and scratched.

Later, for a time, Gabriel was quiet. His brother sat beside him and held his hand.

There is this about families: when one is ill, when one
is frightened, when it is not safe now and here, there is
a place to go back to where it was safe. The brothers spoke
of nursery days. Once Gabriel had thrown a fork with such
determined force that the tines quivered in his brother's
thigh. Once William Michael had overturned a mug of
broth into his brother's water-colours.

"I meant to," he said ruefully, now.

"I thought you did."

Once the milkman had found Gabriel, at four, at an
accurate drawing of his rocking horse.

"I saw a baby making a picture!" that astonished man
had said.

They laughed and for a moment Gabriel's hand clasped less fiercely. But surely as the tide his distress rose again and came crashing, and he spoke of Robert Browning.

"*Fifine* was written solely to hold me up to ridicule."

How does one convince somebody of the unflattering fact that the greatest of living poets probably does not give that much thought to him?

"And Carroll," he said scornfully. "As he prefers to call himself — Lewis Carroll has been a guest in my home, yet to placate my enemies, directs against me *The Hunting of the Snark.*"

Yet Dr. Maudsley had said not to contradict him. So gently William Michael tried again to lead him back to the days when all good things were probable and an impatient world awaited the wonders of the gifted Rossetti children.

"And when we went to the zoo," he said, "Christina always wanted to release the animals?"

Gabriel said, "My raccoon died last week. I wonder how Lizzie managed it."

Outside the high windows the long June evening faded; a faint breeze nudged through the curtains and touched Gabriel's wet brow. The bare walls, the white counterpane, promised to hold the light and failed. Gabriel's rough hair was dark against the pillow slip; his painter's nails, rimmed with bright oils, lay listless. His eyes were hot as coals.

"She has never forgiven me," he said. "She holds me guilty of the child's death — God help me, I think she thinks me guilty of her own."

And now the panic in one brother's eyes met only panic in the other's.

"She hates what I have written. Much, she misunderstands. She thinks I spoke of her when I spoke of Janey." Then Gabriel started from his pillow. "Oh, William! —

Better all life forget her than this thing,
That Willowwood should hold her wandering!

His eyes dulled and he sank back again. "I do not know which woman I meant," he said.

As wary as a traveler who wills not to dislodge the avalanche, William Michael rose from the bedside slowly as he could. It was time — he feared past time — for the paraldehyde.

Alone, Gabriel lay and listened. They would gather in the next room, but he would hear them through the wall; he must have been insane to think they would not sniff him out. He heard them cackle, he heard their obscene mirth; next from that cacophony would rise a single voice to threaten and to taunt: she would have arranged it all.

His breath came shuddering. He strained for the first scuttling, the first mew. But what he heard was his wife's own voice.

Quietly, almost conversationally, she said, "Murderer."

She stood in the corner by the open window, her long gown made of light like the light curtains; her long hair, flaming in the flame of the setting sun, boiled around her shoulders. The green eyes glittered in her thin, white face. And then she smiled, and her pale palms fluttered out to him like doves.

And archly, lovingly, coaxing, she spoke again. "*Murderer!*" said his wife.

So Gabriel Rossetti rose from his bed, withdrew the full bottle of laudanum from underneath the poems that had lain with Lizzie in her grave, and drank it all.

26

H<small>E DID NOT DIE</small>, but he lay like one dead for forty hours and when he awoke, he was another man.

William Michael sold off the animals and the blue porcelain and turned away the servants, and everyone thought Fanny Cornforth would leave too, but she didn't. After awhile he began to paint again, and buyers to buy, but his paintings were like pictures of his paintings; his colours were coarse and the swollen throats of the women goitrous. All his songs were sung.

The others?

Christina never got over the loss of her early beauty; as her lovely eyes protruded, her skin greyed, and her hands trembled, she did not want even the servant girl to see her. Though an acquaintance did once report meeting a little old lady dressed in black who, offended by someone's literary views, arose and announced, "I am Christina Rossetti!"

Pears Soap bought John Millais's painting of a di-

aphanously clad child blowing soap bubbles, and he grew
even richer. Holman Hunt won the Order of Merit. The
dear Old Brown lost a gifted son. Ruskin grew querulous
and peevish; he was in love with Rose LaTouche but could
not marry her because she was ten. Swinburne, in the cus-
tody of Theodore Watts-Dunton, rhymed about babies
and was allowed one glass of beer a day.

But first, Hughes died and Fanny Cornforth married
Schott; they kept the Rose Tavern at 96 Jermyn Street and
kept three in help — but that did not mean she ever left
Rossetti, and she made it clear to Schott before ever they
stood up. No, she was there when he needed her to scold
and cosset and cajole, and through a hale old age she
treasured a note he had sent her: "Dear Fan, do come to
dinner. Do pray come at once."

Gentle reader, it is true that Fanny never understood
him; she thought his pictures pretty and his verses rum,
but she loved him all her life, though he was not a man
much comforted by love.

And she was not with him at the end.

He had been most unwell and his family, falling back
once again upon the salutary ocean air, had spirited him
away to the shore. But there, dispirited and gloomy and
wearing a black glove on the hand that was partly para-
lyzed, he fled away from them at Birchington-on-Sea. It
was Easter Sunday of 1882.

Shortly before he went, Gabriel's black eyes blazed and
he begged, "Don't bury me near Lizzie!"

So one may say that, in a way, she won.

As, in a way, one may say Fanny lost.

For the family was naturally not desirous of the em-
barrassment of her presence by the grave, and William
Michael gave much thought to insure that his answer to
Fanny's anxious inquiry should arrive too late.

Dear Madam, he wrote. *Your letter of the twelfth only*

reached me this morning about nine. The coffin had been closed last evening, and the funeral takes place early this afternoon. There is nothing further to be done.

But Gabriel would have let the old Elephant come.